FOR RICHER, FOR POORER

The Yorkshire Saga Series
Book Two

Valerie Holmes

SAPERE
BOOKS

FOR RICHER, FOR POORER

Published by Sapere Books.

20 Windermere Drive, Leeds, England, LS17 7UZ,
United Kingdom

saperebooks.com

ISBN: 978-1-912786-75-6

Chapter 1

Autumn 1815

Jerome Fender rested his head on the back of the wooden settle. It had become hard and uncomfortable. Feeling the warmth of the inn's open fire offered him little comfort. He downed the end of his tankard of porter and stood up.

The room was becoming crowded. Poorly uniformed men laughed and drank. The food, basic but nourishing, could not be served quickly enough as the newly returned soldiers sat and shared their joy at being home, the reality of their memories etched into their faces.

Boys had left and men returned, aged before their time. Jerome wanted to share in their merriment, but the noise and stench of smoke, the stale sweat of bodies pressed close and the heady smell of ale was so overpowering he had to leave. Good-naturedly he patted the men's shoulders as he pushed his way through the crowd to reach the doorway to the cool of the night.

A woman linked Jerome's arm as he passed by her. The loose neckline of her dress revealed her ample bosom as she leaned into him. "Not going so soon! Why not come and celebrate with me, sir?" she said, her eyes impishly winking at him, but his stomach clenched. They were tired eyes — her body, like her dress, unclean.

He smiled back at her. "Not tonight, thank you," he said casually.

"Your loss." She snapped the words out as she pulled her hand away and pushed back into the crowd to find her next target.

Jerome's hand released the coin he was going to give her, dropping it back into his pocket. She could earn it instead, he thought, and give some other poor sod the pox in the process, no doubt.

Breathing the fresh cold air into his lungs, Jerome rested against the wall of the old inn. He could still hear the drunken banter echoing within, but to him it was as a cacophony of peace. These noises were far removed from the sounds of canon shot ripping through screaming bodies, or the cries of death. He rested his eyes a moment, trying to blank out the horrific visions he had seen; visions that haunted him.

Jerome tried to savour the familiar country smells of the North Yorkshire market town of Gorebeck, replacing the memory of the burning smoke that seemed to cling to his nostrils, or worse, the smell of blood and death. His mind was being slowly cleansed of the hatred that he had heard pouring out of men's mouths for the past five, lonely, years.

Gorebeck had changed so much since he left, with its line of new fine houses following the course of the river that divided it in two. Only the old stone bridge and the Norman church at its centre seemed to unite the two halves — one obviously had benefitted from new money and wealth, while the other, belonging to the poorer townsfolk who had supplied men to fight, had been left behind to fall into disrepair.

What was it the recruiting sergeant told the young men who he enlisted? "A battlefield was where camaraderie and honour was at its highest. There was no nobler cause but to fight for justice and freedom!" How the man had lied and woven false images into his words — naïve boys and delusional men alike had believed them and taken the King's shilling. The battlefield was a deafening, mind-blowing place, where a soul could be destroyed. Those who returned home now needed food and jobs, but both were scarce or expensive; you cannot eat empty promises.

Jerome had been one of the 'lucky' ones — he had survived. He had means. The town was filled with momentary celebrations, the realisation that the men were back in England, in their homes, but tomorrow when the euphoria faded and reality hit, the mood would so easily change. Revolution was feared, like in France, and yet government taxes kept the cost of the very basics of life — the corn prices — high.

Looking across the chilled market square and up the newly laid road to the bridge and the church beyond, Jerome longed for one thing only: to find his true love, a life-partner to cherish. Someone who would share his lonely moments, remove the pain of feelings of isolation and fill his home with warmth. Someone, whoever and wherever she was, who would hold him like they needed him.

A man and his woman stumbled out of the inn, nearly into him. Jerome straightened and surprised them.

"Night, sir," the man slurred as he half-heartedly saluted Jerome, and then the couple laughed and continued, happily swaying in each other's arms as they walked along the street to their home. That man had the companionship Jerome yearned for.

He stared up at the few stars that glistened down. His mother wanted him wed too, but he needed more than a finely bred lady who would add more wealth to the family coffers. There was a growing desire within him — to be truly needed as Jerome Fender. But that woman, if she existed outside of his dreams, would have to be very special, because he was worried his heart had hardened so much that he was now unable to experience real love. How would he ever keep a young maid interested in him by holding refined conversation, when he had returned from a bloody and brutal war? A fleeting memory of trivial parlour games and the habits of polite society flitted through his mind and made him shiver in disgust.

Now he had set his task, he was going to find her, this elusive butterfly bride who would flit into his life, love him for who he was and not what he had, and stay with him for the duration. He laughed. "God, almighty!" he whispered under his breath, if his men knew what had become of their battle-hardened captain they would mock him mercilessly. Next he would be writing verse and reading the love sonnets of the great bards.

Jerome knew that his own family would think him completely mad. His mother would never understand that, with his education and inheritance, he craved to be free of it all. Jerome wanted to own a small portion of land, growing crops to feed his family; it was a romantic notion, yet his dreams had kept him sane in between the insanity of battles. It was in that moment, as a revelation broke through his thoughts of what he had considered was possibly the first signs of madness, that Jerome saw her approaching.

The young maid walked towards him like a faerie in the night. Not his 'butterfly' but certainly a sight to behold. Her fair hair was neatly swept into a bun at the nape of her neck, topped by a small bonnet barely covering the curls that threatened to escape from its side. She held her head erect, not exactly confident, but strangely proud. She looked cold, but was wrapped in a woollen shawl, which she nervously allowed to slip off her shoulder as she approached him, revealing a thin muslin dress beneath.

Jerome watched her approach with interest, taking in her slight, yet curvaceous contours. Was he so desperate for female company that at the first sight of any wanton wench his mind began to romanticise? He had definitely been away too long. It was a wife he sought … not a whore, no matter how comely she may be. Jerome sighed and let out a slow breath, watching the vapour drift away. She was a pretty one and fresh of face, definitely not a woman who had been working the night for long. She crossed the cobblestone road to stand boldly not two feet from where he propped himself against the wall of the inn.

"What's your name?" Jerome Fender asked as she stopped and looked at him cautiously. Her words of reply formed a gentle mist as she spoke. She must be so very cold, he thought. He was, and he was wearing a lined greatcoat of some quality.

"Miss … I mean, Parthena, sir," she said in a delicate voice. It was polite; gentle, not heavy with the rough drawl of a local inn wench as he had expected.

Under the glow of the oil lamp that swung gently above the corner of the inn, illuminating its name — The Hare and Rabbit — Jerome stared into her rich blue eyes.

"Parthena," she repeated again.

Jerome looked at her, intrigued, as her face tilted up to meet his gaze, her eyes heavy lidded, her cheeks flushed. She played the innocent maid well, he thought, but no wench approached a man in the street at this late hour of the night unless they were out to earn some pennies by selling their bodies.

"You are?" she asked.

Jerome hesitated. She spoke to him as if they were meeting in someone's parlour or an assembly room. Very well, he thought, he would play along. "Mr Fender, Jerome Fender."

She nodded politely at him and hugged her shawl closer to her. "Mr Fender, I have only just arrived in town … earlier this day and ... I was promised work, but the family who was to employ me had moved on, so I tried finding employment in the mill outside of town, but they are full as it has been taken by returning soldiers and now... I have nothing and I could not find the priest for he is away..." She blinked. He was unsure precisely what she was wanting.

"Oh, you'll have no trouble finding work in there... A beauty like you!" he said, whilst watching her reaction curiously. "You'd have plenty of offers inside. At least five more men returned today and there'll be more tomorrow, and the day after and for the foreseeable future. You could be kept busy all night if you wished it."

Her expression registered his words with shock. "I need help. I have nowhere to go and I thought that you, perhaps, were also looking for..." Her words drifted off into the night's cool air.

This wench was either very clever or stupidly naive. If only she knew his heart was no longer a soft caring one. At one time he would have taken in the plight of waifs and strays, but he had seen too many for too long. The world was now full of grieving lost souls, or so it seemed; wenches who had followed their men across a continent in a war they had never imagined, to be widowed and left forced to find another to care for them, or worse, take anyone who needed relief. Then there was the plight of women left in captured villages. That was a sight he wished he could forget.

"You have not been in there," he nodded to the inn, "and asked for their help yet?"

"No, sir, I was too scared to enter on my own and I..." She swallowed, and he noticed that her hand was trembling slightly as she pulled her shawl back upon her shoulder.

"You meet some unsavoury characters out here too. Not all soldiers act as a gentlemen should." He smiled and placed a hand on the wooden frame of the back door to The Hare and Rabbit.

"Like you are, sir?" she said. An anxious tremble entered her voice. She was either genuinely in diminished circumstances or a damned good actress.

"What do you want? To whore yourself with me? Is that your trade?"

He heard her gasp and she stepped backwards as if he had physically struck her. It was at that moment when his heart was telling his head to reach for her and retract his words that two soldiers pushed the door of the inn open and continued their brawl out into the street. Jerome was momentarily knocked against Parthena. He grabbed her shoulders and she held tight to his waist. They had to cling to each other in order to balance and not fall in the fouled street. Jerome spun her around away from the doorway as onlookers poured out jeering and egging the two drunken soldiers on.

"I'm sorry," Parthena said, as she gripped him. He pulled his coat around them so it formed a layer of warmth enveloping them both, trapping their body heat inside like a protective cocoon.

"It was not your fault," he whispered into her ear and could have sworn that he sensed a waft of lavender water. She steadied her body against his, but straightened as soon as she regained her balance and composure. He, somewhat reluctantly, let her go.

Parthena quickly grabbed her shawl, which had slipped to the ground, her hands gripping it tight as she took another step away. Her eyes still fixed on his; she hardly blinked as he held her gaze. Beautiful eyes, they were striking in the bright moon glow. Jerome saw her mouth moving before he realised she was still trying to tell him something, but the noise of the crowd drowned out her words.

"What did you say?" Jerome shouted to her, his arm outstretched, willing her to take hold of it and re-enter their cocoon. He would like to feel her warmth again, to be held and to… "Do you want to go inside? I will get you some food and we can talk away from this commotion," he shouted as she continued her retreat. "You do not need to fear me. I can help you."

"No… I'm sorry," she shouted back at him. "I will repay your kindness… I promise!"

"Wait!" he yelled. A cheer went up. One man lay face down in the dirt, groaning, the other had his hands raised high in exaggerated and stumbling victory.

Jerome could not cross the street after her as part of the group jostled to return to their drinks. When they had it was too late, she had turned and run away, lost into the darkness of the night.

Jerome went back inside the inn. Whoever this 'Parthena' was, she was gone and perhaps it was for the better. He could not take on the cause of every deserted wench. His own problems were more pressing. Should he go back to the 'civilised world' of London to have his mama scout for a suitable match for him, or stay in the area and try to find a woman he could truly love by himself? If she came from Yorkshire, his mother would try and disown him. He grinned. It was almost worth scouring the streets of York to find one.

The next morning shone no more light onto Jerome's predicament. He decided to ride out to clear his head. It was only when he put his coat on and ventured outside, curious to see if the faerie of the night reappeared in the daylight hours, that he realised his coin purse was missing. He sighed and tried to retrace what he had done the evening before. He clearly remembered standing outside the inn, gazing at the stars with his hand in his pocket holding the purse. Then he remembered the woman coming to him, like a vision. Next the fight broke out, pushing the inn door open wide with a clout that bound him and the faerie together in his arms. He definitely remembered the warmth they shared, when realisation dawned upon him.

What was it she shouted into the night? Yes, of course her words made sense now. "I will repay your kindness... I promise!" She promised! "The little whore!" he spat out. He would find her if he had to cross every dale, forest and moor to track her down and by God she *would* repay him.

Chapter 2

After taking Mr Fender's coin purse Parthena collected her bag from its hiding place behind the stable and made her immediate escape. Only once out of the vicinity of the inn did she stop momentarily to pour the coins into her hand. It was in that moment that she discovered how large the debt was. Parthena was gripped by such an overwhelming feeling of panic that she froze, staring at the coins. She had been expecting no more than a few pennies, or at most a couple of shillings to fall into her palm, but not crowns. She could be hanged or transported for a lot less.

Parthena collected her things up and kept running until she was beyond the town's reach, or so she hoped. The noise of the night's celebrations were changing to the hoots of an owl, the rustle of trees and the boom of the thumping of her own heartbeat. What had she done? Her pace quickened as her father's face appeared in her conscience. "I'm sorry," she whispered to him as she climbed the steep lane that led onto the moor road. She glanced back down at the lights that flickered, illuminating the town as if the new arrivals did not wish to sleep. She balled her fists knowing it was no use blubbing like a guilty child — she had committed a willing and serious crime on a returning hero. She had made her choice. She had to act with conviction, or else she would truly be lost.

She reached the top of the rise that led to the ancient milestone she was looking for. It was more than a marker of distance along the roads for the coaches and wagons, it was the place where she would find the open moor trods to the village, Beckton, in the next dale. She knew the path well from her childhood. If God's blessing was upon her it would take her an hour, maybe a little more; if she hurried she would be there before the night froze over and she perished. Though why would God help her now? She was a poor sinner and would repent of it when she was safe again. As a child in the Abbey School in Gorebeck she had helped the Sisters move their produce from their gardens over the moor path to Beckton Abbey. There, she, the Sisters and a few other of the girls in their care would rest and spend the night in the cells before heading back the next day to the school where they would have their lessons interspersed with helping to mend and make things for the nuns to sell on again at market.

In between these enjoyable but hard pastimes she was taught the basics of her language and numbers and, of course, the scriptures. She had learned many practical things. Her embroidery skills may have been simple, yet she could make gloves, hats, and clothes. When she was finally allowed home from the school in the summer months, her father had taken a very different view of things when she had told him what she had learnt to do. He had felt the palm of her hand, looked at the tone of her skin and grimaced. In that one moment her life's path changed. Father decided a more refined finishing school was required; and so she was moved away.

With renewed urgency in her stride Parthena stepped onto the trods. It was foolish to risk the path across the moors alone at night. What if the flagstones had been removed and reused? She carefully picked out each uneven stone, glad that it seemed they were still there. As she walked she quelled the growing feelings of panic inside her by planning how she would take up a respectable position, perhaps start her own small enterprise to recapture her previous post in life. She had to keep moving at speed to keep the cold at bay, control her fear and make this crossing the quickest she had ever done it, praying with all her heart as she went.

Her immediate need was to keep herself warm. Taking out her pelisse from her bag she put it on and wrapped her two shawls over the top of her bonnet and her shoulders for extra protection against the night air. With now gloved hands, Parthena carried her bag and continued along the stone pathway that ancient monks, long since dead, had used centuries before her.

She hummed songs, recited poems and texts from the Bible, anything to keep her mind and body from numbing. The irony of doing so was not lost on her as she had broken one of the sacred commandments — that of not stealing — which she never would have thought possible. She swore she would repay the money and never have to break another one. If God helped sinners then she was one, but her cousin had been one first. He had lied to her and sent her on a wild goose chase in order to rid himself of the obligation of providing her a home. She would see justice done, though the law favoured him.

If her father was looking down on his errant daughter now, what would he think of her? She chose to be called a thief rather than becoming a whore! Her loving, intelligent father had not seen fit to trust a female with her own money settled upon her and so had allowed her cousin, Mr Bertram Munro, to squander it at will and send her further north to take a governess's position that did not even exist! Thank God in heaven, Parthena thought, that she had been educated at a school in the same area, or her situation would have been completely hopeless.

Her anger fuelled her progress and provided an inner warmth. Her cousin had betrayed her father's trust in him. How could she regain what the law would not acknowledge was rightfully hers? She sighed, tears of frustration stinging her eyes. The path had levelled for some time whilst her mind muddled through everything that had happened. Now, thankfully, it was beginning to descend. Her body ached, exhausted. Tempting as it was to leave her burden on the moor she clung to the handle and plodded on.

For a solitary moment when Mr Fender had fallen against her, she had been lost in the warmth of his coat and realised how near she was to slipping deeper into his embrace: the touch of another human being, one who was being kind and seemingly caring for her appealed. Yes, for a split second she had considered doing the unthinkable and offering herself up like some form of sacrifice, but she had seen his valuable fob watch and remembered the life she had enjoyed before her father had died, only a year since. Parthena could never hope to recapture it, not as a young woman from a good family, but she could find money if she made it herself. She had an enterprising spirit and had seen how the nuns made things to create funds to sustain the abbey — she could do that and train young girls also to the task. If she threw herself at the first decent man she found in the street, what would become of her? She would find and repay Mr Jerome Fender with interest as soon as she was able — that she promised herself.

She stopped for a fleeting moment and stared at the abbey through the trees in the distance. Then as her body shivered she made one final exhausting push to finish her trek. So long as she kept to the flagstone pathway, she would find her way straight back to the abbey, and they would give her shelter for a small gift that she could now offer them. But if she ventured off this ancient path, even at this last stage of her journey she would be lost in the bog and no one would ever find her, and then Mr Fender would never be reunited with his money.

Daylight was hours from breaking as Parthena made her way down the track from the moors towards the abbey at the southern edge of the town. It nestled amongst a small woodland, sheltered from the wind on three sides by steeper ground leading to the moor above. You could easily pass by this sanctified place and not even know the small community of nuns existed, which was most likely how it had survived so many years when many other abbeys in the region, like Rievaulx, Whitby and Byland, stood in ruins.

Exhausted, and now shivering with the exposure to the cruel elements Parthena stumbled through the ancient iron gates and into the well-tended gardens. They had matured and grown in the years that she had been away. They obviously supplied all the nun's needs, replacing the Abbey School. If only her old school had still existed she could have gone there. She hoped upon hope that one person who had not changed at all was Mother Ursula as she stumbled towards the large locked door. With the last of her strength she lifted the heavy knocker and announced her presence with a clang that resounded as if it would awake the dead. It seemed an age before someone came, but when they did the door that she had not realised she had been leaning on gave way and she made her entrance.

The nun screamed as a stranger fell at her feet. Parthena tried to mutter an apology, but her world spun and she felt herself lose consciousness.

Chapter 3

Jerome's training had made him a light sleeper and an early riser. He made straight for the stable and saddled his horse ready to leave but decided to make one last attempt to find the wretch with the flighty fingers that had stolen his purse. He noticed that the local blacksmith was also up early working so he walked his horse over to the forge.

"What can I do for you, sir?" the man asked without taking his attention off the metal he was hammering.

"I'm looking for a woman," Jerome began and smiled as the blacksmith's expression revealed uneven, stained teeth in a broad grin.

"You are in the wrong place, my man," he answered, before paying Jerome more attention and adding, "sir."

"You misunderstand; I am not looking for just any woman but one in particular who was on her own last night. Fair wavy hair, swept up on her head, slender, upright stance, wrapped in a woollen shawl that matched the colour of her eyes." He stopped himself from adding that they were the most striking, beautiful blue he had ever seen. Even by the subdued light of the moon they had made quite an impact on him.

"Aye, I'd seen her in the street yesterday, then again last evening, looking a sight more anxious about something. She'd be flustered, I'd say, but I don't know no more." The blacksmith removed the hot iron and slammed his hammer down onto it again, his attention back on his task. Then he paused, mallet raised momentarily. "She'd asked about a house. It had been sold on and the people she was looking for had upped and left long ago. So I suggested that she go to the mill and ask for work there. It's two miles or so out of town, yonder," he nodded the direction. "I thought they might take her on, but as I said, I saw her last evening looking edgy like, so perhaps she struck out there too." He smashed the hammer down then turned around and forced the metal into the flames using his other hand to work the bellows. Grateful for the information, Jerome left the man to his task.

Jerome rode out the two miles to the watermill — the obvious place where the runaway woman could have gone to seeking work. This one had ceased to quern flour; it now had weaving machines working relentlessly within it. Cotton and flax had been a cottage industry for decades, providing the local population with an income in the area, where flax was spun and woven into lengths of cloth by families in their homes. Some people praised the new manufactories as places of vast progress and profit, others saw them as fodder for a revolution to the cotton industry — hated for the demise of the local traditions and employment. Still, a mill life was a lot better than the workhouse for those with no way to make a living from the land, Jerome supposed.

He cantered to the edge of the town and took the road that led to where the river flowed fast as it descended through the forestry to the village. Had she too taken this route? No coach had left the town and no one had seen her hitch a ride on one of the few wagons that had left since last night. She could not have simply disappeared.

As Jerome approached the mill he could already hear the clattering of machinery inside and see the smoke from the chimney. All was busy as he entered between the ornate iron gates where the name Beckton Cotton Mill was written out. Jerome tethered his horse's reins to a hook outside what looked to be the main offices. He entered the building and ascended the half dozen wooden stairs that led to the panelled door of the gatehouse and stepped inside the pokey office. A sturdily-built man with a balding head, round face and glasses was busy penning figures into a ledger and he did not look up or acknowledge his visitor. Jerome approached his desk, standing as close to it as he could without actually leaning over.

"If you seek work, wait outside," the man said without glancing up.

"I certainly do not. I seek information!" Jerome snapped.

The man replaced his pen in the ink pot and looked up at Jerome through his horn-rimmed spectacles. "What can I do for you, sir?" he asked.

Jerome smiled. He had no wish to antagonise the chap any further. "I am trying to find the young woman who came here yesterday seeking work."

The portly man removed his glasses and looked at him through tired grey eyes. "We had three young women arrive yesterday and two the day before. These are hard times, sir. Which one is it you seek?"

Jerome described her as best he could. "Slight of build, wearing a shawl, bonnet and about five feet in height. She has striking eyes."

"Aye, sir, there was a pretty little thing came here yesterday in a bit of a flummox. Claimed that she had expected to be a governess for a respectable family, but that correspondence had been delayed and she had missed their departure, or some such tale. Her story had some validity to it as she had the address of one of the families who had rented one of them big new houses in town, sir. I'll admit she spun her words well enough to be credible and knew how to talk fine."

"So did you tell her where she could go for help or offer it yourself?" Jerome asked, confused as to why the woman had come to him so desperate and so late in the evening.

"I am not the parish charity, sir! She may well have fallen on difficult circumstances but what use is a governess in a mill where graft is menial and hours long? They'd laugh at her as she tripped over every stray bobbin. I could offer her nothing other than my condolences and good wishes for another position to turn up, and so she left." He shrugged and replaced his glasses. "Hard work would do her good, but not here."

"Did she give you her name, or say where she was staying or going next?"

The man sighed. "I am not sure of it. Why do you wish to know?" He looked at Jerome curiously. "If you know this woman, how is it you do not know who it is that you seek?"

"I am trying to help her, but first I need to find her." Jerome stared at the man. It was not a lie, for he had every intention of showing her the error of her ways and in so doing he would help her to be a better person.

"Munro... Miss Parthena Munro. That is all I know of her. I am a busy man, sir, and if I should say so she has to find her own way in life as we all do. Good day, sir." His head turned back down as his focus returned to the letter he had been writing. Then he looked up suddenly as if a thought had just struck him. "A word of advice, sir... If you don't mind my being so bold?"

"Go on." Jerome stopped and turned back.

"There are many tales of heartbreak waiting to be heard — regiments have been reduced, hardened veterans discharged in favour of the fresh-faced youngsters who the army keep, and each begging for help, but if you help one, word gets around and then how are you going to help them all? Believe me; walk on by, especially from the ones with striking eyes. They act like lures to decent folk. Wenches will always find themselves a warm bed. Worry more for the men who cannot find work after risking their lives fighting Boney abroad."

"Where did you serve?" Jerome snapped back at him, barely covering the sarcasm in his voice.

The man looked up sharply, his colour deepened. "We cannot all go to war, sir! My heart is not strong enough." He shifted uneasily on his chair.

"Nor is it the heart of a soldier. I have just returned, so I am very aware of the reduced circumstances some of my own men find themselves in. But if I can help one soul before they too fall foul of our times, I will." Jerome did not want to begin a debate, yet he could not stay silent and be preached to by a man who sat too comfortably in his own self-righteous seat.

The man nodded. "Very noble of you indeed. No offence was meant," he said. "It helps, though, if the victim has striking eyes, I dare say. Good day, sir." He looked back to his work.

Jerome did not bother to respond. He had a name, Miss Parthena Munro, and knew her description, but nothing else. How then to catch his elusive, light-fingered faerie?

Jerome left the mill and paused as he reached the crossroads — the town had a road leading east back to Gorebeck. He could continue exploring the small mill village, or he could take the western road which would lead across the Yorkshire Dales to the Pennines. The moors were treacherous and no doubt impassable unless you were a sheep or a shepherd, so surely she would have taken the road. Instinct told him to head for the next village: Beckton. It was nearby, and from there she could possibly pay her way on a coach to the coast. If she made it as far as Whitby and caught a boat down to the

Thames she would be lost to him. However, if he saw her on the road, or if she had boarded a coach he'd have her because his horse could go faster than any public vehicle.

Jerome breathed in the morning air and smiled. The hunt had begun.

Chapter 4

Jerome's mood turned as bleak as the weather as he doggedly rode beyond the junction that led back to Gorebeck. Exposed to the elements, the clouds had obliged him with a soaking. The water dripped off the rim of his hat so he lifted his collar high. "Onwards!" he said, as much for his own benefit as for the horse's as he kicked the sides of his mount and cantered off along the open road. He was already drenched so what was the point of taking cover? Besides the sense of freedom as he charged along was strangely invigorating. For once, he was not pursuing or being chased by a bloodthirsty enemy.

Jerome slowed as he saw a vehicle up ahead skid into trouble. The driver had clearly lost control of his chaise. It veered to the left and then abruptly to the right. There was no stopping it and he heard the screech of a brake being applied followed by a loud snap of wood, the screamed curses of the driver and the frantic neighs of the animal as the right wheel skidded off the edge of the road and into the boggy ground at the side. The horse was pulling in panic to keep the vehicle and itself aright and its efforts had stopped the whole thing from falling onto its side. The driver jumped down and Jerome dismounted and fought to help the man steady the distraught animal.

"Hold him fast! I'll attach it to mine," Jerome shouted through the rain. The driver did not argue, gladly accepting the help.

Once held, they managed to pull the chaise wheel free of the quagmire, using the power of the two horses together as they guided it out and set it straight.

"I'm afraid one of your spokes has been dislodged," Jerome shouted to the man, pointing to the splintered wood.

"I'm grateful to you," the man replied, as he came around and inspected the damage. "It was good of you to stop and act so quickly."

"We can force the wood tentatively back, but without hammer and nails it simply will not hold. You will need to ride your horse. I would not try sitting on the chaise if I were you."

"Aye, I know that. You are bloody lucky, man. You only have the horse." The man shook his head and wiped the rain from his face in a fruitless gesture.

"It's still damned awful weather for the descent," Jerome said. "His hooves are not that sure."

"Aye, but there's nought stopping you cutting across the moors. I have no chance with that," the man answered as he hitched up the chaise to the horse again and climbed onto its back.

"If I had a death wish I would," Jerome answered, looking over the boggy moor.

"Not if you kept to the old trods," the man replied, smiling when he saw the bemused look on Jerome's face.

"I have lived in the region for years; I know of no such paths." Jerome rode alongside his new associate, his interest piqued.

"You see yonder milestone?" The man pointed about fifty yards further up the road as they walked their horses onwards.

"Yes," Jerome nodded.

"Well, that also marks the pathway across the moor and into the forestry down to Beckton. It cuts off miles and you would be sheltered from this bloody awful weather. On foot, donkey or horse you can use them, but it's a single flagstone path, not one for wagons or carriages. Monks used them for centuries."

"You are certain they still exist? I wouldn't find myself stranded mid moor?" Jerome asked as they approached the milestone.

"Nope, that you wouldn't, sir, they are still in regular use, but not by the local gentry."

Jerome turned his horse to the stone pathway that had emerged before him, disappearing into the mist of heavy rain. Could the young woman, if she knew the area, be brave or bold enough to try such a journey? It was beyond his comprehension that a woman who was of gentle breeding could take such a treacherous path — but she was a desperate one. Then again, if she knew the area that well why was she walking the street at night? Why did she steal? There was only one way to find out. Jerome dismounted and led the horse along the uneven pathway, craving the shelter of the forestry to come. He kept his eyes fixed on the worn down stones. It was true they were passable but over the many years of use some had sunk or become slightly overgrown, making them slippery.

By the time Jerome had found the shelter of the trees, the storm had abated somewhat. A dark thought had crossed his mind and he was mightily relieved not to have found the woman's corpse. It had been a strong possibility that, if she had been foolish enough to try this pathway, she may have succumbed to the elements.

He led the horse through the trees until he could see a pathway down into the town. There was no sign of anyone having passed this way recently. Jerome could make out an old building through the treetops to his right. The horse needed warmth and dry stabling to rest and feed, and he a room at an inn and a change into dry clothes. He had survived battles in the soaking wet, but did not wish to risk his health over some personal quest. Once he had his accommodation sorted, and a hot tub made ready, he would eat his fill of food and continue the hunt.

Jerome's instinct was telling him that the meeting with the driver on the moor road had been significant. When timing worked in your favour, it was a beautiful thing; you just had to keep your eyes and ears open for an opportunity. It could turn the fate of nations when it happened in battles. That nameless man was meant to send him on the right path and yet, comprehending that his thieving faerie could know of this trod, or be bold enough to take it, seemed beyond his reasoning ... yet she was bold enough to steal his purse. So ... who knew?

The rain continued to lash down as Jerome reached the town and no one was on the streets. Holding his hat with one hand, he steered the horse towards the shelter of the stabling at the back of an inn. He could not read the sign as it swung in the gusts of wind, but as he approached the buildings a lad came out and offered to take the reins. Jerome released his bag and ferreted inside for his other coin purse and passed the lad a few pennies. "Tend him well!" Jerome shouted over the sound of a crack of thunder. The lad nodded as he led the horse away.

Jerome burst into the inn. His mood was as foul as the weather. What a wench can cause a man to do, he thought bleakly. Seeing his reflection in a narrow pane of glass as he entered, he wondered who was more foolish, the runaway woman or the dupe who gave chase in such weather. He stopped momentarily, removing his dripping hat and giving his eyes time to acclimatise to the gloom. Faces stared at him from cosy dry seats. Ignoring them, he walked straight over to the serving hatch, adding more water to the already soiled threshing that covered the flagstone floor.

"Best of the day, sir! What can I get for you?" the hoarse voice of the serving woman asked. Her smile was spoiled by her browning teeth and strong breath as he neared.

He smiled back at her, trying to lift his mood. "A room, a hot tub and a clean bed would be fine, but first I need a good brandy."

She winked at him, pulled a bottle of French brandy out from under the counter and poured him a decent measure. Strange how when facing the elements Jerome had not been so aware of the cold, but now as his body warmed he felt it and shivered involuntarily. Eagerly he drank the brandy and replaced the empty glass on the counter.

"Sally, make a room ready for the gentleman and have young Jeb fill up a tub for him by a warm fire," the woman shouted without looking behind her, her eyes fixed instead on his wet, cold figure.

There was a scurry of activity behind the woman as the lass and lad appeared from the back store room and went about their chores.

"Anything else?" the woman asked, obviously happy to have some new custom on this miserable day.

Jerome glanced around the poky room and saw the locals take up their drinks and continue conversations, his presence apparently uninteresting enough to hold their attention — good, he thought! He downed another drink in one gulp. "Yes, you can help me further," he looked at her and leaned nearer wanting to keep his quest his own concern, "I'm looking for a woman."

The serving woman raised her brows. "We run a respectable house here," she said and blinked coyly. She leaned forward to meet his gaze and her bosom seemed to swell as she rested it on her arms, exposing more of her cleavage than he wished to see. "However, for the right price we can arrange … most things…" she added.

He half smiled, a strange feeling of repulsion creeping up from the base of his stomach. Looking at the hopeful eyes of the 'mature' woman who flirted with him now, it was all he could do not to swallow back his words and run. "Sorry, I misled you … unintentionally of course." He smiled. "I meant that I am looking for a specific woman."

"Another drink, sir," she asked, standing straight again and holding the bottle up waving it slightly.

If he wanted information it would cost him. "Yes, and a hot meal would be welcome after my tub, but I am looking for a Miss Munro. She came ahead of me arriving on her own as I was delayed, and I was rather hoping that she may have already taken a room?" He smiled and held his glass out for another drink, knowing that she would take some more coin from him one way or the other before she was willing to help him. She poured another brandy and he drank it, realising how much he also needed food in his stomach; it was feeling very empty.

"Sorry, sir, no woman is staying here by that name or any other. We have a couple of officers, a mill owner and a priest. They're all waiting for the coach to take them on to York, but none have a single woman with them."

"When will that leave?" he asked.

"Tomorrow, at midday. But it's fully booked so there will be no space for her on that. If she's in town, she'll be easily spotted." His face must have showed his disappointment. "Mind, she may well have gone to the abbey for a bed. Depending on what sort of lady she is." She winked at him. "The more virtuous kind don't tend to stay on their ownsome in an inn, even one as respectable as this."

"Could you make enquiries for me?" he asked. He placed some coin on the counter but she laughed at him.

"Don't think I'd go near a place like that! I'd be struck down!" She continued to laugh, a raucous coarse noise that made him smile to hide the cringe he felt grow inside his cold and hungry gut. Eyes looked around but then they returned to their own business. Her cackle must also be a common enough sound to their ears.

"I may well be a bit obvious myself." He tilted his head on the side as if to look appealing — for he was sure she would be able to find out if she really wanted to.

"Well…" The woman glanced at the ceiling and sucked her browning teeth as she rubbed her thumb and forefinger together.

He placed a further coin on the counter and kept a finger upon it before she could pick it up.

"Are there any other inns in the town?" he asked.

"Aye, one at the other end in the old part. I doubt she would go there, though. It's positively ancient. Wooden floors warping, and the damn place falling apart around the guests' ears, not like our good establishment here. This one's built to last."

"You make a good point." He released the coin. "Have someone make enquiries discreetly. I will double it — if you locate her," he said.

"Good as done, mister." She winked at him again. "Now you relax and take off that sodden coat before my next customer has to swim over to be served, eh!"

Jerome nodded and slipped off his coat before taking his weary body up the rickety stairs to his room. He would take his rest, warm up, eat and, when the rain ceased, he would see if they had found where she was. If not, then before he left this town he would take a walk through the main street of Beckton, look out for her and ask if she had been seen anywhere — including the old inn. His horse needed to rest anyway and dry out as much as he did, but his determination to capture the thief had grown with every uncomfortable hour he had passed in the saddle.

He was used to harsh conditions, but never had he been so easily duped in his life before. Why should he care what happened to this woman? He wanted his coin and that would be the end of it … except for those memorable eyes haunting him…

The following day brought no more sightings of Parthena. Jerome had combed Beckton and talked to vendors and the other innkeeper, but no one had seen hide nor hair of his elusive butterfly.

Returning to the inn, he decided he may as well leave the next morning and try picking up another trail. She cannot have got away, other than on foot, without someone spotting her … unless she had gone to one of the many isolated farms and asked for help. If he asked around those he could spend weeks scouring the area. He needed a sign to show him which direction to go in.

He crossed the tap room of the inn deciding it would be better to be on the road again looking than wasting time here.

"Ah, there you be…" the serving woman called over to him.

He stopped and decided a drink before he left might be in order, but then realised that she was more animated than she normally was. Hope raised its head again.

"You have some news for me perhaps?" he said as he put a coin down on the counter. She filled a small glass with brandy and slapped her hand down beside it.

"Aye, Bessie doesn't let her customers down. Your wench arrived in the dead of night at yonder Abbey." She folded her arms; a smug smile beamed back at him.

"The old building in the trees?" he said as he swigged his drink down in one. He could hardly believe that he had been so near to her hiding place and had been on the verge of leaving her there and moving on. His sixth sense must have been exhausted by the time he reached the village.

"That be the one," she said and smiled. "Who is she then? A runaway bride? You chasing her are you?"

"No, it's not like that. I'm only trying to help a friend in trouble."

"Oh, aye. I bet you are a regular Robin Hood, eh? Well your wench is holed up there and, if you take Bessie's advice, you make sure you put on your sweetest voice and most believable tale of woe if you want her released her into your care. The Sisters ain't easily fooled over there."

Jerome put another few pennies onto the counter top. "My thanks for your help. I may need the room another night or two."

"You're welcome," she said, but as he left he heard her laughing.

Chapter 5

Parthena awoke. A shiver ran through her as she moved and her body ached. Her mind was numb. She stared at a stone ceiling and felt a coarse blanket over her — no, it was not a blanket but the rough shift she was dressed in. A feeling of alarm grew as she realised that she was in a cold stone cell. The mattress she was lying on felt lumpy, but at least it gave some warmth.

Parthena looked down to the stone floor tiles and saw a chamber pot sticking out from under her bed. That was what was making her feel so uncomfortable; she desperately wanted to use it. Once she had emptied her bladder, she stood and stared around her. She cringed, remembering the communal buckets of the dormitory that served the same purpose, and worse, when it was her turn to empty them. Deciding she had had enough of nostalgia, Parthena looked for her bag, and spotted it hanging over an old three-legged stool in the corner of the room.

She rummaged inside it and found her brush and comb. Pulling on her dress she then combed out her hair and swept it into a bun before placing her bonnet atop it. Her boots had been cleaned and left on the floor for her by the stool. Her coat had been laid carefully on top of her bag. How lovely it was to see the sign of another person's effort on her behalf. There was a time when she had a maid to come to her when she called, who, Parthena realised, she had viewed as one of her possessions. What a price that woman had paid for Parthena's comfort. Strange as she looked around this barren cell, with only a crucifix for adornment, how she had never thought about such things before. Now it seemed to Parthena that she was, in some way, turning into a different person. She saw the value in every small aspect of life. In fact, she now saw the value of life itself. Never would she ever complain of being bored again. Or realise that to be bored was to throw the beauty of opportunity and freedom back in her good fortune's face. The poor, apparently, had no right to be bored, tired, ill or ambitious. She was not used to being poor and had no intention of being so again. Dismissing the knowledge of the source of her money, she pulled on her coat and boots and collected her bag.

Parthena grabbed hold of the large iron door handle and tried to turn it. It did not move. She tried again. It was only when she really pulled and tugged that fear replaced her moment of joy for it was obviously locked and bolted. She felt an overwhelming sense of panic. Had she been found out already? Was this sanctuary a prison? Had the man come looking for his coin? In that moment she had never valued anything more in her whole life than that which had just been removed from her — her freedom. She dropped the bag and began to hammer on the door with both fists.

She knew how thick the walls were and how long the corridor was. This place had been part of her childhood for all too short a time, but it was etched in her mind as much as her own home. Soon she heard feet running toward her cell and she grabbed her bag tightly to her; it represented all her worldly possessions. She tried to think quickly of a plausible way to explain her actions. If the man Fender had found her, her life or liberty could be forfeited for her crime. She now wished upon wish she had just run over the moor to the Sisters and begged for their help when first the trouble had happened. But how could she now undo her act of desperation?

Parthena wondered if her only escape was to join the Order. If she confessed she had no doubt they would put the money she had stolen to good use and keep her in repentance from now until her dotage. She was not prepared for that, neither was she ready for the transport or the noose. She would have to find Mr Fender and repay him but she could not face the long trek back across the moor. Her head swam — she had not eaten, and her thirst was intense. She clung to her bag even more tightly as the door opened; her mouth felt dry and the room moved around her. She was fortunate that as two Sisters entered the room they realised she was about to fall again and grabbed her to stop her from collapsing on the stone floor.

"My dear!" one exclaimed as Parthena was steadied. "Come with us, you have rested plenty, but now you need to eat." Parthena felt the bag being taken from her hand as she was frogmarched out of the cell, heavily supported by her two escorts, down the side of a cloister. There was a cool breeze that caressed her face and awoke her senses.

The smell of the food seemed more acute than it should be as she entered the hall and watched the Sisters having their broth and bread in a neat row at tables lining an old stone arched room. The vaulted ceiling was high and the air around her was unnaturally cold, despite the warm food being served up.

No one spoke, but she was escorted to an empty space and a Sister gestured that she should be seated. With her bag placed close by her feet Parthena climbed in. It took little persuasion for her to consume the barley-based broth and as it slipped down her dry throat she felt her energy return. Grateful, she finished her meal and, using the bread, left the bowl wiped clean.

"You must come with me now," one of the nuns said to her the moment she had finished, stepping back ready for Parthena to stand. Her bag was taken by one of the others. No one else spoke. They silently stacked their bowls as she left. Eyes watched her, but no one gestured or smiled at her.

Parthena followed her escort around the stone corridor to the corner of a quadrangle, the middle of which was being used to grow small crops of herbs within the shelter of the walls. An older nun hoed it lovingly, completely focused on her task. The place had a beautiful feeling of timeless peace about it that stilled Parthena's anxious heart. They stopped where stairs spiralled up out of sight behind the ancient walls. Here the nun stepped aside again and allowed her to climb them first. Parthena thought of refusing, feeling as if it could be a trap, but she wanted to see Mother Ursula, who she knew sat in the office above. How old would she be now? Parthena wondered if she held the same affection in her heart for the young 'Thena' as she had for the old woman. She followed the curve of the stone wall, carefully placing her feet on the small worn steps that had many a foot fall upon them over the centuries. When she came to a wooden door at the top she knocked and waited momentarily until a strong female voice ordered her to "Come in!". It was certainly not the fragile voice of the elderly Mother Ursula.

Parthena placed one hand on the large iron handle, while her other hung by her side, missing the comforting weight of her bag with the stolen coin hidden inside it. She swallowed, almost feeling as if the sin of her crime could be read in her eyes as she entered. Peace had vanished again and the burden of guilt gnawed at her soul instead. The room was stark. A woman sat behind a desk on a simple chair. There was no fire in the hearth behind her and no hangings covered the bare stone walls. The wooden floor creaked as Parthena crossed its uneven surface.

The woman watched her, but did not speak until Parthena stood before her.

"Your name, girl," she said.

"I am sorry to have inconvenienced you and would like to offer you a…" Parthena began.

"Do you have a problem hearing me, or simply comprehending my question? I asked you what your name is." The woman's back was straight as a broom, her eyes piercing.

"Yes, I heard and understood your words well enough. However, I was going to offer you a donation before I left." Parthena looked at the hard face of the lady opposite her. Her manner was offensive, but she was nowhere near as old as Ursula had been.

"Who are you running from, girl?" the woman continued. "You came here two nights hence…"

Parthena gasped — she had no idea how much time had passed by. No wonder she had been so thirsty.

"I see you have little understanding of how much you needed our help. You arrived at our door just in time. If you had collapsed outside in the forest or on the old trod you would have perished." The woman stared at her. Parthena wondered if she had compassion in her voice or merely judgement of Parthena's apparent stupidity.

"Would half a crown be sufficient for your kindness and hospitality?" Parthena answered. She was beginning to feel trapped again and had no wish to be incarcerated here, or in a gaol. She turned around and took the bag from the nun who had stood silently behind her holding on to it. She opened it and as quickly as she could found the coin she sought and offered it up for the woman to take. Instead, the Mother Superior slowly sat back in the chair and stared at her.

"We gave you the room and board free of any charge. We are not running a boarding house here, or a shelter for waifs and strays as they pass by. I take it from this you have no wish to join our order as a novice."

Parthena swallowed. The desire to take to her heels and run was very strong. Was the woman toying with her or serious? She was a hard one to read. "I merely sought shelter. If it was freely given then I thank you for your charity and ask that you accept this as a donation for your good work, so that you can help another who needs it and who is unable to offer payment of any kind."

The woman gestured for Parthena to leave the silver coin on the desk. She did not handle it herself. "So, tell me who it is who turns up, desperate, at our door and then offers to pay handsomely for our hospitality."

"I would bid you good day," Parthena answered and turned to leave, but her exit was blocked by the other nun, whose ample figure all but filled the width of the doorway. She made no attempt to move, but folded her arms and stared at Parthena with a slightly raised brow and challenge in her attitude. One finger gestured that she should about turn and face the Mother Superior again. Parthena felt intimidated — she wanted to protest, but the last thing she needed was more trouble or suspicion thrown upon her.

Parthena swallowed and turned around. "I merely wish to leave and not trouble you any further," she said and smiled as sweetly as her tired face could manage. "You have not given me your name either."

"You never asked me, but my name is Mother Melissa and I merely wish to know who it is that has slept under our roof, who was in my care and who now wishes to depart in such a hurried fashion, leaving a considerable sum behind them." She leaned forward, her voice slightly gentler, but the look in her eyes just as intense.

"My name is Miss Parthena Munro. Now may I leave?" Parthena held the woman's gaze, but cursed her own stupidity — she had just given her real name; had she no sense left in her addled wits? But then this was a house of God, how could she lie and expect Him to protect her as she bumbled along on her present path of seemingly self-destruction?

"From where did you come and why did you not go to the inn for rooms with such coin in your purse? Why straggle in the gloom of the night and not hire a horse or chaise?"

Parthena realised she had arrived as a mystery to be solved — a truth to be discovered, someone who had disturbed their solitary and peaceful lives. She also thought that Mother Melissa may well have rifled carefully through her bag to find answers in case Parthena had not woken. "I had an unfortunate experience. I was supposed to take a position of governess in Gorebeck, but found that the family had moved on by the time I arrived. Messages and letters had apparently crossed. I was left with nowhere to stay and nowhere to find suitable alternative accommodation."

"This family were not here in Beckton, but over the moor in Gorebeck?" the Sister behind her persisted.

Parthena did not bother to turn around so she answered the woman's question directly to the Mother Superior. "Yes, it was a respectable household over in the village of Gorebeck, not here in Beckton Dale." Her voice had an edge to it as her anxiety was returning. She had to take a breath and calm down. They had every right to be suspicious of her.

"You cannot have walked all that way by road — who helped you? A passing farmer?" The woman sat forward. "Have you any idea of the danger you put yourself in? Could you not use your money to catch a coach to wherever you originally hailed from?"

Parthena looked at her and decided to tell the truth — almost. "I walked over the old trods from Gorebeck to Beckton. I was at the Abbey School as a child and crossed the moors when the supplies were taken to market. I'd remembered it from back then. The school does not exist now, but the trods have existed for centuries."

Mother Melissa smiled. "You have nothing else to tell me, Miss Munro? Am I correct in assuming, because of your persistence to leave, that you have no intention of considering staying here?"

"Yes, with no disrespect, I wish to leave," Parthena stated emphatically.

"Very well," Mother Melissa said and nodded to the Sister behind Parthena who opened the door wide.

"Thank you," Parthena said, and took a pace forward before freezing as a gentleman stepped into the room.

"Do you know this man?" the Mother Superior asked.

Parthena swallowed. "This is Mr Jerome Fender. I have met him once and indeed he has helped me from a fate worse than any I had previously encountered in my life. I owe the man thanks for my safety." Parthena stood straight and tried to keep the wobble from her voice as her body trembled from within.

"You are indeed fortunate, for this gentleman has told me he has travelled all this way to come here seeking you out so that he is able to help you in your recent plight."

Parthena stared at him, not understanding if there was a game of words being played out around her or if he had really not told them that she had stolen the money from him. "Have you, Mr Fender?" she asked. "Is it your intention to help me and put right the grievous wrong that has befallen me and has seemingly drawn you into it as a result?" Parthena was surprised by the confidence within her own voice.

"I would be most interested to hear of your grievous wrongs, but perhaps we could leave the Sisters in peace whilst we ascertain the depth of your problems. I do not see any point in involving them further…" he replied, not taking his eyes from hers. "Do you?"

"Is this your wish, Miss Munro?" the Mother Superior asked. "Are you content to leave here with Mr Fender?"

"I should not bother you further," Parthena replied and swallowed again because her head and her heart were giving her conflicting advice.

"Once you depart here you realise that you will be beyond the protection and sanctuary of the abbey and my power," Mother Melissa added.

Parthena nodded her understanding, but could not put into words her thoughts because they were scattered to the four winds. She was following her instinct again and yet doubting it was a reliable ally.

Mother Melissa then addressed Jerome. "Mr Fender, you swear to me on the Holy Bible that you will take care of this lady and see that she is safe from harm's way. Whatever her circumstance, I believe it is not of her making, and would ask that a secure place of employment or a safe home be found for her, when you leave here."

He nodded his agreement. "I give you my absolute word that I will see she is well cared for." He looked straight at Parthena. "You have my oath on that, lady," he added.

"Then leave with my blessing." Mother Melissa waved her hand and the nun opened the door wide. Time for talk had ended — Parthena had made her choice and the future was beyond this enigmatic woman's reach. Now she had to step out into the world with a man who she had previously robbed of a small fortune.

Chapter 6

Parthena felt her whole body shake as the ancient wooden abbey door closed behind her and the clang of a metal bolt resounded as it was firmly replaced. The minute they stepped outside the abbey grounds Mr Fender cupped her elbow with his hand and took her bag from her. Parthena snapped out, "Unhand me!" as soon as she felt his grasp but her words were met with another sudden jolt. Shocked by his abrupt action and his touch she almost cried out to be allowed back inside the abbey, but she had made her decision — Mother Melissa had made that quite clear. He spun her around to face him and one word stilled her. "Silence!"

She glared at him and was about to make further rebuke for manhandling her, but he shook his head slowly.

"Say one word, Miss Munro, and I will call in the local militia — their billet is not far away and you are no more than a common thief, and possibly even less! Or, if you prefer, I could find out where the local magistrate resides and simply take you directly to him." He glared down at her and she bit her lip, knowing he had right on his side.

Parthena felt shame like she had never felt before and tilted her head down so that her bonnet would shield the high colour in her cheeks. They burned as the guilty feelings that swept through her soul scorched their path into her heart. She pictured her father's face and had to quash the tears that she could feel building up. How far she had let him down.

Without lifting her head to meet his accusing face, she spoke quietly in her defence, "I can explain. I promised to pay you back. I…"

"You will say and do nothing until we are in a place where prying eyes are not watching us. You can then tell me your whole story, and though I have no reason to, and little understanding of why I am prepared to, I will listen and judge you accordingly."

"Who are you to judge me?" she responded, lifting her chin, and realised how foolish she was, for he had the law on his side and she none of it.

"I am a barrister, woman! You thieved from a man who has spent years studying the law of the land before he went to fight for it, and I am repaid by being the victim of a common cut-purse."

Parthena tried to stand straight and not buckle under this new twist of fate... A barrister! She would not beg or plead but she had to try and make him see reason. "I am not common, nor am I a cut-purse. I think that is why you are prepared to listen to me. You know there is more to this, to me, than that. You see it and sense it. I merely borrowed the money because the alternative was far worse and I wanted to... I intended to repay it..." She understood that she was at his mercy and whim. Yet, if he was a fair man then he might just help her.

Jerome walked her over to the side of the abbey wall where a chestnut mare was tethered to the rail. It was then she had her first clear look at his generous mouth, framed by a determined jaw. His features were accentuated by deep brown, sad eyes. His looks were not grand in a Romanesque way, but in strength of character — a man who had seen many things, worldly and still very much in his prime. He dropped her bag to the ground and placed one hand firmly at either side of her waist, gripping her through her pelisse, and lifted her bodily to place her sideways onto the saddle. She let out a gasp and grabbed the saddle to keep her balance. He said nothing while he placed her bag on her lap. She had to hold on to it with one hand and the horse with the other.

"Tell me, in your desperation and generosity, how much did I give to the abbey for your board?" he asked.

"Half a crown," she replied in a quiet voice.

"My ... how generous I am for two nights' stay in what will have been a cold cell, no doubt!" He climbed up behind her, flicked the reins and with a slight jolt they were on their way to where? She had no idea.

She sat with her back straight and looked at the road ahead of them. Mr Jerome Fender was a man of the law! Could she have chosen a worse person to steal from? She stared at the sky from under the rim of her bonnet and prayed that he was truly a just man, for she needed one to dig her out of the mess her cousin had thrown her into.

"Where will you take me?" she asked, swallowing so hard that her mouth had gone quite dry. She thought of the prison cell she could be thrown into with goodness knows who: men and women together, possibly. Did they keep them separate by gender, rank or by crime? Parthena had no idea what the rules of prison were, but they would be harsh and she would have no things of her own, for her crime was not because of debt, but a true crime of theft. She had stolen money — and a lot of it. Society would have most likely thought more of her if she had used her body to earn it. A tear ran down her cheek as he answered her question.

"Miss Munro, you will come back with me to my room in the inn. There you will explain what possessed a woman trained enough to be a governess to steal from someone who had offered her help. For now, say nothing. The woman in the inn will presume you are my whore and I do not care if she does. You have cost me enough. You will accompany me to my room and there you will answer all my questions. If you choose not to then I will take you to York myself and lay a formal charge."

Parthena turned her face to look down at him. "Would you do that to me after … knowing that I was a governess?" she said quietly.

"Miss, even murderers can be gentlemen, vicars and politicians; they still have to answer for their crimes. You stole — you broke the law and you had no right to call it a loan when we had no agreement. Now, be quiet and be grateful that you have the opportunity to come with me at all."

She felt his body's warmth close to her. He wrapped one arm around her waist. Parthena held on tightly to her bag as the horse moved and she found it a steadier option to hold his arm tightly with her other hand. Propriety had left when she had fallen foul of the law. Now she had to survive and stay out of prison.

Then a thought crossed her mind: if he was a barrister and he knew the law he should be interested in seeking justice. He could possibly help her. Had she not been wronged by her cousin? Had he not sent her on a wild goose chase and no doubt hoped she would never return or recover from the shame of it? A flicker of hope lit in her heart, but it was a very small one that could so easily be extinguished. Mr Fender might take pity on her circumstance and seek out her cousin.

They did not go far before Jerome rode into the stabling area of an inn. Silently he dismounted and helped her down to the ground, all the time keeping a firm hold on her. The woman serving did not look surprised when he came back in with her at his side.

"Found her? Ah good! Would she want food and a tub too?" she asked.

47

"No, I'm fine," Parthena said quickly. "I've eaten, thank you."

"Yes, she does, both," he said, completely ignoring her words.

The woman smiled, baring her ugly teeth and Parthena wished she could turn around and walk out. But she could hardly run to the abbey again. She had rebuffed the Mother Superior's offer for her to stay there so she had made her bed — and now she might literally have to lie in it. The thought made her shiver as she looked up at the tall frame of Mr Jerome Fender. Would he expect her to lay with him? A flood of emotions she did not recognise rose within her, almost squashing her immediate reaction of pure fear.

He had muttered something to her, but lost in her own thoughts she did not hear him. Not repeating his words he cupped her elbow and pushed her firmly in front of him so that she had to go up the wooden stairs first. They approached a door that he quickly unlocked before steering her inside. The room was sparse, but there was a warm fire and the tub was being filled by a boy and a girl who were running up and down the stairs with pails of warmed water.

"Won't take long, miss," the girl said. "We always have water on the fire for the laundry. Sally does it in the tub house out back."

Parthena wanted to offer to help them and run away, but she knew she had to face the battle to come. He had chosen his ground, but she had to somehow win.

Chapter 7

Parthena and Jerome waited in silence for the last two pails of hot water to be poured into the tub. A rough piece of soap was placed on a tray on the floorboards and a cloth for Parthena to dry herself with, but no chemise was left for her to actually bathe in. Jerome passed the girl and boy a coin each, which they heartily thanked him for and closed the door after them.

Parthena stood stock still as he then turned and looked at her. "Your bath awaits, Miss Munro," he said and gestured with his hand that she should go over to it.

It was positioned in front of the small open fire. The logs crackled as they burned slowly in the grate. The tin bath had a higher back than front. Jerome picked up the only chair in the room and placed it back to back with the tub. Only a yard separated the chair and the highest end of the tub — even though they faced the opposite directions, it offered little privacy to Parthena who was in no doubt what he expected her to do next. Jerome took hold of her bag and placed it on the floor in front of the chair.

"Miss Munro, my attention will be taken with that." He pointed to her bag. "You will take off your attire, entirely, for it needs cleaning also, and climb into the water whilst it is still warm. Then as you wash yourself you can tell me your sorry tale and, please, do not think to embellish it with falsehoods, or this will be the last wash you will be able to have in any sense of relative privacy for some years to come. Gaols offer few creature comforts and inmates are monitored and watched over as they are checked for lice, illness and all manner of skin ailments that accompany immoral living or poverty."

He stared at her for what seemed like an age. She faced him defiantly but he did not turn away. His words made her shiver. She had heard of people going into the workhouse and being treated like animals, but what did she really know of such things? Her cousin had said some awful things to her in order to gain her agreement to set off on her journey — alone, with the only comfort being a letter, a reference and a guarantee of respectable employment at the other end of her journey. What a trusting fool she had been. Now look at her plight!

"You think I am going to strip down to my chemise ... here, and see to my ablutions with you still in the room?" She began to shake her head, trying to build up the courage to make a stand. "You are mistaken, sir!" she said, her voice wavering slightly. "You may think I am of low morals, but I can assure you that I am not. I am a lady!"

Jerome sighed, walked across the threadbare carpet, pulled the ribbon of her bonnet and tossed it onto the bed. "I do not *think* what you are going to do, for I know it. I am clean and you are not. You will correct that as I listen to your story and you will show some trust in me, as I have absolutely no reason to trust you at all." He sat on the chair, looking down and opened her bag.

"You intend to rifle through my things?" She fought the words he had said in her mind, knowing there was little she could do to resist if he insisted.

"Yes. I intend to review all the evidence before me. Now, take your clothes off and leave them in a pile by the door and plunge in, or I will remove more than your bonnet myself. Do not think for one moment a woman's screams in such a place as this would get anything more than curious glances up the stairs."

"You are no gentleman!" she snapped, and slowly removed her pelisse.

"As you are definitely not a lady, I am not sure how you would know," he said and looked at her. "Continue to remove every stitch. You smell, you have been on the road too long and I can see in your eyes how inviting that water is, so please carry on." He then turned back to the bag.

Parthena had too much pride to accept the situation, yet not enough courage to deny him and face the consequences. Every word he had spoken was true. She stood at the opposite end of the tub. Her eyes were firmly focused on his back lest he should turn around. As quickly as she could she slipped out of her garments and into the welcoming water and felt it caress her body as she slid under its spell. Closing her eyes she let her head dip under the water level so that the roots of her hair could be massaged by her fingers as she cleaned it. When she sat up, trying to keep as low to the water level with her knees tucked up to her naked breasts, she heard him speak. For one fleeting second she had started to enjoy the bath and had forgotten he was there.

"Now, Miss Parthena Munro, begin talking and I would know the exact truth, no embellishment and no untruths."

Jerome was soon sure that her bag held few secrets. She had a letter of introduction written for her by her cousin, thanking Mr Bartholomew Squires for offering Miss Parthena Munro a place as governess to his two sons. It seemed genuine and would have sufficed along with the reference from a Reverend Dilworth stating her good character and her family's pedigree. She was obviously well connected, yet this had not stopped her being turned out by this cousin, Mr Bertram Munro. It was not an uncommon situation for a single young woman to find herself in. Parthena's future was dependent upon the goodwill of her nearest male relation to arrange for an introduction to a prospective husband or find her a position.

If what she was telling him was true, this cousin had sent a young woman, unchaperoned, to a house which the people had apparently moved on from before he had even written the letter. He began to understand how desperate she must have been. He had glanced to his left. The looking glass above the table in the corner of the room offered him an unexpected and very pleasant view. Her exquisite lean body slowly captivated his vision. Jerome's mind told him what he should be doing, but a very different part of his anatomy was telling him what he wanted to do.

He stared back at the bag in front of him, closed it and controlled his breathing, and repeated the word 'Thief' in his mind to dampen any desire he had for this woman... It was not only her eyes that were captivating.

"Did you honestly think that you could get away with robbing a total stranger?" he asked, his voice slightly husky.

"I did not think. I did not know what else I could do. If I asked for charity, with all the men returned from the war, I would have been laughed at, or worse, taken advantage of. They were not going to offer me help; they would have offered me warmth for a night. Or perhaps a few minutes intimacy."

"I did," he said. "I said nothing other than I would help you."

"I thought you were offering me something that I could not accept," she said quietly. "I had sunk low, but not..." Aware of the water cooling and her nakedness she stood up and stepped out, wrapping the piece of towel around her body and dabbing herself dry by the fire.

Jerome had looked at the looking glass and watched her, but quickly turned his head away again as he took no joy from her discovering he had seen her in the flesh, although he could think of many a way that he could find joy with her, for both of them, if she were willing. The thought warmed his usually cold heart.

Parthena asked him to throw her clean chemise from her bag and a dress. She watched as he produced the chemise but was horrified when he walked over to her and handed it to her personally.

"The dress ... you forgot it... I have a day dress I can change into." She pointed to her bag. "You must have seen it."

"Wear that and slip under the covers of the bed and warm up properly." He flipped back the bed cover.

"Do you intend to take advantage of me now — is that it?" Her eyes were wide with fear, but as he stepped right up to her, with only a thin fabric between him and her body, she was feeling more than fear. He placed one finger under her chin, tilted it up so that her lips were almost touching his as he leaned down to her. She could feel his warmth, smell his musk and sense his desire. He kissed her ever so tenderly, his lips lightly brushing hers.

With the fire warming her back and his intimate touch, she was confused, but before she could look away he suddenly stepped back and smiled at her. "Do not flatter yourself so much, Miss Munro."

She had to face away, ashamed.

"I have business to attend to. You will stay here and await my return. To venture downstairs would be a big mistake."

Parthena glanced over her shoulder; she doubted she could feel more shamed than he had already succeeded in making her. It was all her own fault — well she blamed her cousin first, but her actions of late had been of her own making. She watched as he picked up her bag and headed for the door.

"You can't take that!" Fear crept up her spine at the thought that his repayment for her dishonesty might be to desert her there, leave her penniless and near enough naked in such a place. Did he seek her total ruination?

He bent down and collected the dress she had taken off as well. "Yes, I can. I intend to for your own good."

"But what am I to wear?" Panic threatened to overwhelm her. Her legs and were folding and buckling beneath her — he had surely won. She trembled as tears welled up inside her.

"The chemise, I told you. Now slip into bed and do not venture outside of the room. You would definitely not get far in here dressed like that. I will be back shortly."

"Will you?" The words slipped out of her mouth as a desperate plea and he paused. Her question hung in the air and momentarily he did not answer her. A tear escaped her and trickled down her cheek despite her resolve not to show weakness.

"You will have to learn to trust me, as I did you." He could not look her in the eye and left.

Jerome did not intend to go far. He could not risk Parthena running again or her being discovered. She was a soul who needed saving, but she was also desperate and that desperation had already led her to commit an act of great folly. Fortunately it had been against him and not another returning soldier. He asked the girl, Sally, if the laundry she mentioned could clean Miss Munro's dress and undergarments. He then booked the room for a further night.

"Food for the young miss?" the serving woman asked, as she held forward a pewter plate on which something resembling stewed pork and turnip had been poured. It looked warm, not enticing, but it was sustenance after all.

"Thank you." He took it. For a moment Jerome stood there holding her bag in one hand and the plate of food in the other. He shook his head and carried both back up the stairs. He had intended to teach her a lesson, but those beautiful eyes had moistened and, despite her brave efforts, she had cried. He could not do it. Whatever wrong she had done him, another wrong added did not make his actions right. Instead, he returned to her, rather than let her fear him anymore.

He dropped the bag to open the door. As it opened wide, Miss Munro stood with a blanket wrapped around her. She was beautiful; she would have been wasted as a mill-worker or a governess.

"This is for you." He pushed the bag inside the room with his foot and placed the plate on the small table at the side of the window. Then he dragged the tub onto the landing where it could be seen to without them being disturbed further. Before stepping back into the room he slipped downstairs, returning with a bottle of wine and two glasses. It was time for them to talk honestly and for him to help her.

Jerome found her checking her bag. She had slipped her day dress on, an ice blue muslin gown that complemented her eyes and her fair hair. That hair hung loose over her shoulders, still slightly damp, but as it dried the blonde wisps only added to the ethereal impression of the faerie he had first seen in the night.

"You are quite beautiful, Miss Munro," he said, and placed the wine and the glasses down on the table also.

"I don't know what you want of me, or to do with me, but please let us be honest with each other as flattery will not soften the blow. Just state what terms you are offering me, if any, for the wrong I have done you to be righted. I know you could have me hanged for I am guilty and I have no defence I can make that will stand in law." She was holding her hands in front of her, turning one anxiously with the other as if to steady them. They were shaking and he saw in that moment how truly scared she was of him, of her plight and of her own stupidity. It was then Jerome knew what he wanted for her and him, but how to win it without her feeling obligated or in fear of him? He had never threatened a woman, and he had no intention of starting now, but she had to truly understand the gravity of what she had done.

"You are bold and brave as well as misguided in your judgement." Jerome lifted the chair over so that she could sit at the small table. He poured the wine and took his and sat purposefully back on the bed against the headboard so he did not crowd her, and sipped his drink, glad of its soothing taste. "You were in a dire situation, Miss Munro. What you did was wrong, as you now realise," he said, watching her poke her food with the spoon.

"Yes, I do," she replied without looking back at him.

"Then let us look into the circumstances that forced your hand, whilst you eat. For I have no wish to have you hanged, pilloried or even chastened for your crime. From this moment on we shall only talk about what drove you to it and what will be an end to your dilemma. I give you my word on it."

Her head shot up. "You do not intend to…" She swallowed.

"I am not a destroyer of young maids in any form of the word. I would gain little by throwing you to the wolves who would relish having you at their mercy inside a gaol. Neither would I stoop so low as to take advantage of a young lady who has fallen on hard times. So, having established those two facts, please trust me, and tell me about this cousin of yours, but eat as well as talk and enjoy the wine, for it is really quite pleasant."

"Thank you," Parthena replied, and smiled for the first time. He saw her composure change and the frightened wench transformed into a more relaxed beautiful woman. Jerome had a heart to win over — hers — for, as he sipped his wine, his thoughts returned to the notion of having a wife with whom he could build a future, and before him he seriously considered the possibility that fate may have brought her to him.

The warmth that swept through his body was not only of the wine's making, but the small kindling of some strange emotion that grew in his heart. A soldier's heart had returned from the wars and he felt alive again — he actually felt a glimmer of joy. He smiled at her. Parthena still looked slightly nervously over to him; he had found what he sought; now he had to convince the young lady that what she had also found was him.

Chapter 8

"Parthena." Jerome spoke again only after Parthena had finished her meal.

"Thena, please," she said as she looked up at him. "If we are to be friends then I would have you know me by the name one would use." She smiled genuinely at him, replacing her previously wan look with youthful enthusiasm.

"Only if you wish it," he said.

"Yes, I do. I insist; after all we are sharing a room." She had lowered her voice but was being coy rather than frightened as before.

"Very well. Now, tell me more of this Mr Bertram Munro, who sent you away from your home." At the mention of that name Parthena's smile disappeared to be replaced by an angry glint in her eyes.

"Cousin Bertram had been to York three months earlier and had met up with some friends, the Park-Hamiltons, who he said had told him of a family in need of a trusted governess who could live in as part of their family in a respectable and fashionable town house. He had met Archibald at Cambridge and said he had bumped in to him from time to time in Boodles in Pall Mall when he was in London. It was arranged, he told me, that they would meet me off the coach, but when I arrived no one was there. I waited, in case they had been delayed, even though I could not understand how they could be. They were the ones that lived locally — it was I who had travelled by the coach — but still no one came, so after an hour or so I made enquires and managed to find their town house using the address I had been given." She shrugged as the rest of the story was known to him.

"I suspect Bertram already knew that you were going to miss them. If he had met them three months earlier, the man would surely have mentioned that in less than a month they would be moving abroad."

"How do you know how long it was since they left, Mr Fender?" Parthena asked. She tucked her hands around her knees, balancing her feet on the edge of the bed.

To Jerome she looked a vision of perfection. When fear left her, her persona changed and he could sense her inner calm. She had a happy heart, one that had been tested and troubled of late but that shone with innate good nature. He hated this man Bertram for what he did to her, yet in a strange way he owed him also, for without his evil actions Jerome would never have met Parthena.

"I asked around. It is obvious what he intended to happen to you, Thena. Otherwise, why ever would he have sent you away without a chaperone, with no person to turn to if the journey had not gone well?" He leaned forward and placed his empty glass on the table next to hers.

"Bertram had initially meant to come with me, or that is what he told me, but his gout played up and he was unable to travel. Then Reverend Dilworth offered to see me to the coach. He stayed long enough to make sure that I was seated safely and waved me off."

"Or, perhaps he just made sure you left on it," Jerome added, deep in thought.

"But he is a good man — my father trusted Reverend Dilworth. He has been in the parish for more than fifteen years." Parthena turned her chair to face Jerome. "Surely I should be able to trust a man of the church, Mr Fender. If not, who can we trust?" Parthena stared at him.

"Who knows what tempts men," Jerome commented without making further accusation.

"Can I ask you … did you mean what you said earlier?" Parthena said directly, her cheeks flushing slightly.

"About helping you — yes." Jerome swung his legs onto the floor so that he was sitting opposite her, their knees almost touching. "I will not report you, my word on it. Now, you must put that behind us as I have." He was puzzled when she began shaking her head.

"I thank you for that and I accept your word on it, but I was referring to your comment earlier — what you meant when you said that I would be flattering myself to think that a gentleman such as you would want to touch a person such as me?"

Jerome took her hand in his and lightly held it.

"I wish only to know what you meant… I'm not offering…" Parthena tried to pull her hand out of his, but he gently held on to it.

"I meant to offend you; it was beneath me, and it appears I have succeeded. Forgive me that one ill thought-out comment, for it was a cruel slight and could not be further from what I actually wanted to do. Believe me, you are a beautiful young lady and one that I suspect has been wronged, morally, if not legally. So I have arranged for us to stay here one more night and tomorrow we shall catch the York coach. From there we will rent a chaise so that you can return to your unsuspecting cousin and see what he has to say to you when you face him, unannounced and unharmed."

"How will I explain your presence?" Parthena asked curiously.

"You will not, Thena. For I intend to call upon your cousin as a visitor, after I have collected some more facts. You will say that the family had left, as he presumably knew they had, and that you were generously provided with the ticket for the coach by your old friends at the abbey. Make no further embellishment of the story, because when the truth is to be bent, it is safer to bend it in the fewest words. That way lies cannot be determined and unpicked so easily."

He saw her lift her face and smile at him again. "Thank you," she said, and then asked, "What will I do then, once back in the Hall?"

"I suggest that you behave as if you are quite upset by the ordeal, ill even. Take to your bed for a day to rest from your journeying, but make it clear it is only from the journey and nothing else is amiss and then spend time indoors, out of his way, whilst I make my arrival. It should only be a day or so before I join you. If you should have access to his study whilst he is out of the house, perhaps you could delve a little into his papers and see what his letters can reveal of his plans. Do you know if your father left a will?"

"I was told that none was found, but I did not believe this to be the case as Father was always so meticulous about his business dealings. However, he would have left the estate to my cousin, or my husband if I was married, of that I am certain." She looked away, then stared boldly back at him. "He did not think that ladies were made to cope with the fine detail of business," she added. There was a bitter edge to her words that was laced with guilt, because she obviously had loved her father dearly.

He half smiled. "No matter. We have some digging around to do. Do not mention me, or what you did. That is between us. Now we must find out what motive this cousin of yours has for wanting you out of his way. It seems the Hall would have been his legally anyway, so why was it so important to him to remove you from the place? It could be he has a wife who would not abide your presence; such situations have been known, but I do not understand why he would treat you so callously as to encourage your ruin." Jerome ran his fingers through his hair. "Do you know who dealt with your father's legal affairs?"

Parthena shrugged her shoulders. "He never involved me in anything like that. Even when Mother was alive he was meticulous about keeping anything to do with his business affairs away from the family. He strongly believed that ladies should not have to worry over such things," she said and laughed. "What he could never understand was that we worry more through the not knowing anything of such details."

"Many men do share that view, but I take your point as a very valid one. It is always the unknown that distresses people more."

"Mr Fender…"

"Jerome," he offered.

"Very well, Jerome — why would you do all this for me?" she asked.

"Because I believe in justice as well as enforcing the law of the land. I am for reform, Thena. I do not see why a person should be hanged or transported for the theft of a crust of bread to feed their starving family, their crime being treated the same as someone who stole ten pounds or murdered. Circumstances should be taken into account as well as the crime. There are more people like me who are trying to change our harsher laws. You have told me what had befallen you, and I accept the truth of it. Are we to be true friends?" he asked.

"I think we already are. You are certainly being a far better friend to me than I have been to you. I shamed myself and…"

Jerome leaned forward, stood and gently kissed her forehead as he straightened up. "That is in the past. Now let us focus on the future. We stay here one more night and leave on the morning coach. No fear is needed, you are safe with me. You shall sleep under the covers and I on top. You will be safer in a room with me than one on your own in such a place as this."

"I agree, for purely practical reasons…" she said quietly, looking at the bed quickly, but then away from it.

Parthena watched as he carried the tray outside the room and left it on the floor for the girl to collect. Returning to her, he stared out of the small window that overlooked the stable yard. "I have a horse to see to. Would you care to join me and we shall explore the town of Gorebeck and perhaps find you a new pair of boots? You have all but destroyed those on your cross moor adventure."

She looked down at her boots. They were a sorry sight even though the nuns had tried to resurrect them, especially when seen next to the finer quality of her dress.

"I owe you so much already, Jerome," she said.

"Perhaps, but it is of no consequence. Fate has brought us together, Thena, so let us not fight that and instead work together to unravel the knot of deception your cousin has manufactured. Do not forget I am a man of law. I shall unravel his knots and see you have what is yours by right to have, and if anyone needs bringing to justice, I think it will be him." He paused. "But I cannot promise you that I can have him disinherited if the legal right is his."

"But have you nothing else you should be doing? Are you not a busy man? You gain nothing from all of this unless I can inherit some of my father's wealth in which case I shall repay you tenfold," Parthena commented, and saw a slow smile cross his handsome face.

"I was busy at war — I am no longer. For now I am simply enjoying being 'Mr' Jerome Fender, independent of rank or position. I should be returning to my dear mama who will be desperately wanting to see me settled down in a legal practice, with a society wife, positioned in a respectable home. So you are quite wrong, for I believe I have much to gain by doing the correct thing by you."

Parthena looked quite puzzled by his words. She stood and pulled on her pelisse. "Then I have been fortunate indeed," she answered.

Chapter 9

Parthena stood before the old grit-stone Jacobean building. It had seemed very strange arriving back here in a chaise, well presented and with a wave to her father's tenants, clear for all to see.

Leaham Hall had been in her family for three generations and was her father's pride and joy. His grandfather had saved the life of a lord, and in his gratitude that lord had left one of his estates to him along with a legacy that would keep it going. The legacy, she thought sadly, had not helped her. Her father's greatest sorrow had been his inability to beget a son and heir, but he had always been a loving, caring father to her and never begrudged her anything. Parthena could not believe that he would not have made provisions for her future also, to protect her beyond his own lifetime. He knew that his heart was weakening and had therefore had time to prepare for his demise, so why would he not leave a will? Why had he not left a living for her? She swallowed back unshed tears, for this was her home no more and now she had to face the man who had taken it from her.

The rise of Parthena's anger stopped her from giving into her melancholy thoughts. She raised her head high as she walked up to the front door of the building, and paused. Should she knock, like a visitor, or enter like one who belongs? She smiled; she would be damned if she was going to knock. She turned the large iron handle and swung the door open wide before walking boldly in, dropping her bag on the floor inside the hallway. This was still her home. Yet, it felt different, as if the warmth had somehow left it when she did.

Elsie Hubbart, the upper house maid, was the first person to spot Parthena as she scuttled from the servants' stairs toward the day room. If Elsie had seen a ghost the effect upon her could not have been less dramatic.

"Miss Munro!" Elsie almost broke into a run to greet her. "It is so good to see you here, miss, but I was not expecting you." She took Parthena's pelisse off her as she spoke.

"Why were you rushing so?" Parthena asked.

"Oh, well, in case Mr Munro comes back. He doesn't like servants to be seen in the main hallway and I was, well, taking a short cut." Her colour heightened, but Parthena realised that it was not guilt or embarrassment, more her temper being controlled. Elsie Hubbart had worked at the house from being a girl herself; she would not like Bertram's sudden appearance and highhandedness any more than Parthena did. "Are you on your own, miss? Has Reverend Dilworth returned with you?"

Elsie looked past Parthena towards the open door, staring down the Hall's gardens to the ornate iron gates that marked its entrance and separated it from the road to the ancient village beyond. The short drive led to the main road and the market square of the small village of Leaham. It was a fairly secluded place and pretty as a famous oil painting by Gainsborough in Parthena's eyes. Unlike the harsher reality of the market town she had just left, and the wild expanses of moorland that surrounded it this place was a haven — unspoilt and beautiful with woodland banks and picturesque cottages outside of a peaceful, yet busy village square.

"No, he has not." Parthena was not about to begin explaining what had happened to her to a servant, before facing Mr Bertram Munro. "Take my bag to my room, please. I hope my trunk has not been sent on already. It was supposed to be forwarded when I wrote to my cousin letting him know that all was well and I had arrived safely. He should not have had that letter yet. Unfortunately our plans had to change."

Elsie stared at her, but did not move for a moment as if she was trying to frame her words of response. Parthena now realised that Bertram would have been expecting a very different letter, one that would tell of a desperate woman who had resorted to God knew what existence in order to survive. Once fallen, in any respect of the word, he could cast her off easily, as no one would want to know her — well, none of her previous acquaintances.

If she had not seen those poor people returning from war with no work to go to, or the wretched souls who toiled at the mills, would she have given them a second thought? Her brief scrape with life as a felon had changed her perspective on the world. Something inside her had hardened, her naivety had been removed and as she thought of her new friend, Jerome, her heart welled with gratitude and admiration. He had seen her as a thief, judged her and found her a worthy person. He knew her for what she truly was and he had promised to help her.

Elsie broke into Parthena's thoughts.

"Miss ... we heard no word from you. So Mr Bertram said that the trunk, your things, should be stored in the attic room, I believe." The woman looked quite ashen-faced.

"You believe?" Parthena queried.

"Yes, miss, although Mr Munro was talking of having it brought down again before this weekend." Hubbart had started to wind her index finger in the edge of her apron.

"Where is Mr Bertram Munro now?" Parthena asked. She could not smell the smoke from his pipe hanging in the air and so guessed he was either out or still abed.

"He is in town on business, miss, but should be back by noon." Elsie bit her lip and then blurted out, "He has been busy preparing the Hall, miss."

"Preparing the Hall for what?" Parthena asked.

"Well, miss, we have been told that at the end of the month it is to go up on the market for sale, miss. Everything, the Hall, the land, the tenancies ... everything!" Elsie's voice rose slightly with incredulity.

Parthena stared at her, not knowing quite what to say. Her home was to be sold; without warning, and without her knowledge. She held the gaze of the servant who had served her father loyally for years and felt sad for her also, as well as all the tenants who relied upon the land for their livelihood.

"Sold! But what is to become of you and the staff?" Parthena asked.

"We have been told that we are to hope the next owner keeps us on, and if not, he says we can always look for work in the village. But there is no work in the village and no one wants to leave to go to them mills, miss. So we all hope that we will be taken on by whoever purchases the estate. Mr Bertram Munro has made it very clear that he has no interest in it, although he has been making an inventory of your father's paintings and things, miss." Elsie paused and her words sank into Parthena like a knife. "Perhaps you could speak to Mr Munro on our behalf and ask if we could be accounted for in the arrangements?"

Parthena recognised the tinge of desperation in the woman's voice and understood it. "I will speak to him about his plans when he has returned from his business. Please make my room ready and have my trunk brought back down to it. I would have my clothes back where they belong and aired if needed. Be assured, Elsie, I will speak to my cousin. Let me know as soon as he returns. I would like to surprise him." Parthena forced a smile, feeling more like decrying the low-life who would bring such heartache to her and her home community.

"Thank you, Miss Munro."

Parthena watched Elsie run up the stairs as quickly as her feet would allow her to. Parthena had been turned out as a foolish young girl, but with God's help she had returned a woman with a quest. Beyond saving herself, she now had to take it upon herself to save Leaham Hall and all who depended on it.

Breathing out slowly, Parthena made her way to the library, remembering times spent with her father fondly, and then looked to the adjacent door of his study. If Bertram was not to return till noon there was an hour clear. She entered through the large doorway and stared at the polished walnut desk. It had papers scattered all over it. Her father would turn in his grave at the mess. He had always left everything orderly — always. It was his way. Again, she wondered where he had left the will, for he would have made one, she knew it.

She glanced out of the window to see if there was any sign of Bertram returning, but there was not. Curiously, rather than guiltily, she opened a large folder that was on his desk and read the documents that were to hand, glancing quickly over accounts, bills and tenancies. Looking at the plans that had been drawn she began to understand the gravity of the scheme Bertram was set on. It seemed he was planning on selling off everything. There was a sketch of the river with buildings redrawn by the bend of its course. The river was full of freshwater fish. It was then that she realised that these new buildings were of a mill and cramped accommodation for workers. He planned on destroying the Hall and the farms, and in their place dirt and grind would despoil the natural beauty.

She had to hold onto the desk and steady herself because what she saw was the total destruction of a way of life that was precious to her.

Another drawing outlined a row of slightly grander terraced housing that would face the village square. The older pretty cottages would be levelled to accommodate these. If Bertram had his way this village that had prospered for centuries would become another grubby mill town. There would be nothing peaceful left about it. The house staff would find work, but it would be in a noisy, dusty factory. She must tell Jerome and stop this. How, she did not know, but what of the legacy that went with the land? Perhaps it would have some clause within it that could be used.

Parthena put the papers and drawings back where she had found them. How sick she felt. How disappointed and helpless. But she had the help of a man of law to support her. Mr Bertram's plans were about to discover a few obstacles. She would not relinquish everything her father had achieved so easily. The battle was on, and she had a very capable officer in charge of her campaign.

With that surprisingly pleasant thought Parthena quickly made her way up to her old room. It was very much as she had left it. Parthena could almost believe that time had gone back and her home was hers once more, but time never did that. Her father had said it to her on many an occasion that time can be a good friend or a heavy enemy, it depended how well you used it. They had stood before the grandfather clock in the hallway. It hadn't worked for years, but he had told her he used time well for it was his best friend. She loved his fanciful side, but, like the clock, his time had stopped all too soon.

Parthena prepared to welcome her cousin, grateful to have all her clothes returned to her. Bertram was about to learn that it was not so easy to rid himself of her or the responsibility he owed to the estate workers.

Jerome followed Parthena's chaise to the estate and, once he saw her safely arrive from his lookout place at the end of the short drive, he made his way into the pretty, but sleepy-looking village of Leaham.

Jerome led his horse to the small water fountain in the centre of the picturesque village square and allowed him to drink. Casually, Jerome surveyed the buildings around him. The offices of Messrs. Blackmore, Hide and Stanton, the legal representatives, were next to Farthings and Crutch the undertakers, and he wondered for a moment at the name 'Stanton' which was familiar to him from the Inns. He had studied with a Mr Geoffrey Stanton and taken exams at the same time as him … fate, he mused, could be a wonderful thing if it was working in your favour. Up to now, it seemed to be favouring him well.

He was about to enter the nearby inn when a coach drew up in front of it. The man who alighted made straight for a coffee house. So, letting his intuition guide him, Jerome did likewise. It was then he saw a familiar face, a man seated at a table with another, shorter, man. Both had greeted the gentleman from the coach and had not seen Jerome enter behind him. Jerome slipped into a seat where the high-back settle facing him obscured him from view. He leaned into the corner casually and listened.

"Charles, my good man! Glad you could make it. Please sit down, sir." Bertram's voice was full of gushing greetings. "You know Stanton here," he said almost dismissively.

His guest must have nodded for there was silence but the sounds of movement; Jerome presumed they were exchanging handshakes.

"How was your journey?" the voice continued to fawn; Jerome's gut instinct was to dislike him intensely.

"Not too bad, Bertram. So, tell me, who is your friend?"

Drinks were ordered and apart from hearing the other man introduced as Charles Tripp, Jerome could not hear much more of their initial small-talk as he, too, was served by a friendly young woman.

"No." Bertram's voice rose, then as if remembering where he was he lowered it and continued, "I tell you, she took herself off to some northern Yorkshire market town on the whim of becoming a governess. Miss Parthena Munro is one thoroughly over-indulged young woman who has no refinement or sense of duty. She ranted about making use of her education! A woman indeed! I tell you, I have never heard such nonsense coming out of the mouth of a young lady. She must have been spoilt as a child by the father to have become such a wilful creature. Her mother left her and that is the shame of it, as the man obviously had no idea how to school her in the finer manners needed to fulfil her duties in matrimony. So the burden of the estate has fallen to me. The place has hardly changed since Henry VIII was our king. Mind, there was a man who knew how to handle women!" He laughed. When no one else did, he continued, "I have not heard a word from her since. It is a bad business, Stanton."

"So, where does this leave things, Bertram? Whatever the rash acts of this girl have been, it is of no consequence to our agreement, is it?" Charles Tripp asked. There was an edge of silence.

"Well, as I understand it, the legacy only attaches itself to the direct bloodline if there is a male heir — a son. It blocks an heir from selling the estate on, only if it is passed down the direct bloodline in this manner. So, if there is no son, and no son-in-law to inherit, then the land and all that is on it, goes in entirety to the next of kin, however distant they may be, so long as they are male." Bertram cleared his throat, before continuing in a smug tone. "Is that not correct, Stanton?"

"Yes, it seems so," Geoffrey Stanton replied. "It is, I am sure, not what was meant or intended by the deceased, but the devil is in the wording. However, this lady appears to have acted in haste. She is naive and I am sure cannot have travelled far. Perhaps we should send someone to seek her out. I know of an ex-soldier who is excellent at tracking people who have tried to evade the law. Finding Miss Munro would be easy for him, I'm sure."

Stanton was being very considerate of Parthena, and perhaps he did not agree with all that Bertram was saying. Jerome hoped so, for he could become a much-needed ally for Parthena.

"I agree. If she had stayed and not acted so brazenly, I could be finding her a suitor, but the headstrong, foolish girl has run away and I cannot trace where to." Bertram made a scoffing sound. "Finding her at this stage would be pointless — she is disgraced. No respectable suitor will want to offer his hand to a runaway governess. Unless I palm her off on a willing farmhand! An estate needs a gentleman to run it effectively, not a simple-minded girl, or a social-climbing labourer." He laughed and then broke into a coughing fit. Clearing his throat he continued more calmly, "The address she gave me was false and no one seems to have any knowledge of where she is. Who, of any breeding, would even look twice at her should she reappear?" he asked and then, his diatribe over, sighed. "She has burnt her bridges!"

It was Stanton who spoke out, and it was the next words Jerome heard that convinced him he was definitely the man he knew.

"I am most bemused that she has been so knowledgeable about the world to be able to disappear so easily and completely. However, until we can locate Miss Munro, should we not delay the sale of the estate, lest there be any challenge made by another claimant? After all, is it not possible she may have eloped, in which case she could challenge everything you have planned and her husband could legally try to take control of the place? The will does say quite clearly that…"

"What! Preposterous nonsense! There is no suitor and, besides, her father never bothered her with the details of the will. Why would he? You are thinking strategically; as an educated man, you forget she has the mind of a woman — no more than that of a fickle girl! What challenge could she make? It is highly unlikely that she will announce an engagement, or God forbid, a rushed and shameless marriage, under the circumstances."

"But if she had met a gentleman who could woo her and form such a plan…" Stanton continued.

"No, I am afraid that Miss Parthena Munro, until the death of her father, would have had no opportunity to meet any such person. You overestimate her awareness and knowledge of the situation. Please allow us to do the thinking and you stick to the legalities and paperwork!" Bertram snapped back.

Stanton breathed in heavily and Jerome smiled for he realised that a wedge was now forming between Stanton and his client that could indeed work very well for himself and Parthena.

Bertram Munro was the first to speak again. "The paperwork is explicit and Charles has other options to consider. Do not waste any more of his precious time on such half-baked impossible theories. We must move forward with this swiftly. There is much to arrange and I need to sort affairs out for Leaham Hall and return to Kent. Mother will be most anxious that things have been dealt with satisfactorily. She is a respectable lady and would be horrified if she knew what my new charge had been capable of."

"Indeed," Tripp added. "The girl is irrelevant to everything. Bertram has inherited the estate and we have an agreement as to what will happen to it as soon as you can push the necessary legalities through. Now, I expect the paperwork to be finalised by the end of this month. If it is too big a job for you, Stanton, then I will consult my London lawyers..." he allowed his voice to trail off. "I am sure they would be able to finalise things quickly."

"I think our business is done here," Stanton announced rather abruptly. "I will see to the transfer of the estate efficiently, as is my brief, and will be in touch with you gentlemen shortly." Stanton pushed back his chair further, scraping it on the stone floor. "Mr Munro, Mr Tripp, I bid you good day. I, too, have much to do." He stood up and walked out.

Jerome watched Stanton leave and smiled. Good, they had upset him. He would not have appreciated the jibe about him being inferior to the London lawyers. Stanton had fought prejudice all through his studies as his father's money came from trade, so-called 'new' money. They may now have lost the loyalty of the man they most needed to steer their plan through. If Jerome went to Stanton, with care, it could well play into his hand.

Bertram had obviously not seen Parthena yet, but he was busy painting a very different image of her than Jerome knew to be true. He turned his glass around on the table. What he and Parthena did next had to be carefully thought-out. Bertram was hiding the truth from Parthena, but he had carefully orchestrated things so that it was only her word against his. Had she, in fact, left without his blessing it would cast a very dark shadow over her reputation. The letter she had of introduction to the family, the one he had read, said that she had been sent by Bertram, but it was the only proof she had that he arranged it. Yet, Jerome now realised that Bertram could challenge this as the signature upon it comprised only of two letters — it could be said to be a forgery. Bertram may be full of his own self-importance but he was beyond doubt sly. He could outwit a young woman when he had full knowledge of the terms of a will on his side and his legal right as a man, but outwitting Jerome would be a different matter.

Jerome was about to stand up and follow Stanton outside when he heard Bertram's voice rise again. "It concerns me that my man could not confirm what had happened to her. I expected a report that would give us surety that the girl could be no more trouble to us. Despite her having no other means to survive that are, shall we say, reputable, she managed to completely disappear, Charles. I tell you this has been an ill thought-out affair. We should have been bolder."

Jerome balled his fists and held in his desire to drag the man out and accuse him then and there of wrongdoing — but what proof did he really have of Bertram's intentions? Tripp would hardly bear witness against him. He would back his business partner and it would be their words against his own.

"Bertram, good fortune has smiled on you here; do not cast a shadow over it by tainting it with the blood of an innocent. I will not be party to that," Tripp declared.

Interesting, Jerome thought.

"You said to be done with her," Bertram replied.

"I may have made an offhand comment. You could have sent her to a convent, had her sent overseas to have her education finished, anything — any legitimate reason to send her away. How you chose to interpret my words is down to you, but you have interpreted them badly and the consequences of them will be yours if she emerges as an embarrassment to either of us." Tripp sighed as Bertram made to protest. "Listen, man," Tripp continued, "she will have found a way to survive as we all must. You focus on moving the sale through quickly. I will give you another month and then I expect to be able to bring in my men and start work on this backwater to make it pay handsomely." Jerome heard Tripp move his chair back.

"Yes... Yes ... of course! Everything will be ready. Do you wish to stay at the Hall tonight?" Bertram asked.

"No, I have other business partners to see. I will meet you back here in four weeks to the hour and the day. Have everything ready for me, or I will be forced to buy land elsewhere. Progress stops for no man, Bertram!"

"Of course, I fully understand," Bertram grovelled, as the Tripp left to return to his coach.

Jerome watched as the vehicle drew away and listened to Bertram Munro who was left cursing his business partner and the 'bitch who had escaped his man'. Bertram then headed off in the direction of Leaham Hall, and Jerome almost wished he could be there to see his face when he returned to find Parthena back safe and well. However, he had to reacquaint himself quickly with an old colleague. Jerome stood and walked purposefully over to the offices of Messrs. Blackmore, Hide and Stanton.

Chapter 10

Geoffrey Stanton recognised and welcomed Jerome as soon as he stepped into his office.

"I am so pleased that you remember me, sir. If you recall we were in the Inns at the same time…" Jerome responded.

Stanton shook Jerome's hand enthusiastically. He then took Jerome's hat and placed it carefully on a stand by the closed office door. "I never forget the face of a friend, or in your case, sir, a friendly face. You were always a gentleman, Mr Fender — Jerome, wasn't it?" He gestured that Jerome should sit down in the chair opposite his own desk.

"Yes," Jerome replied.

"I know I am right, sir. I pride myself on my memory of faces and names." Stanton smiled.

Jerome nodded. "An excellent memory, sir, and one that will serve you in good stead in our profession."

"Well, I'll be honest with you, I have another reason to remember you. You stopped Giles Baglan from giving me a kicking in my first term at the Inns. I do not mind admitting to you now that I was quite afraid. I had never been so far from home. I found myself surrounded by buildings beyond the height of any I had previously seen and in a very different world to that of my own simple home town. I admired you from that moment onwards and I have followed your career with interest. Now that the war is over we can pursue our chosen paths once more. I served in the 95th, sir. Only a lieutenant, but I did my part." Stanton held his head high.

Jerome was momentarily speechless, but then he smiled broadly — 'One good deed' was the phrase that came to mind.

They exchanged rank and anecdotes for a few moments with enthusiasm, and then there was a slight pause in the conversation.

"So, tell me, what brings a London barrister all the way to this part of the country?" Stanton took his seat again after offering Jerome a glass of sherry from his cabinet.

"Justice, Geoffrey, or lack of it, that is why I am here. I am for reform, so that the punishments we deliver are more fitting to the crimes. It is something I have long believed in. Those crimes can and should be prevented whenever possible. Sometimes we have to put the letter of the law aside and re-evaluate our actions and the need for discernment in what we do and who we support."

Stanton stared back at him considering his words before responding, "I, too, am for reform, but these things take time, especially where laws are concerned, as well you know. We also have to remember that no one should be above the law or else it serves no purpose and all we do is create our own folly, or break it ourselves." He then glanced out of the window for a brief moment as if lost to his own thoughts.

Jerome was about to break through them when Stanton spoke again.

"I am not happy with how things stand at this precise moment. If I am to be honest I have not been for some months. I have a wife who expects our first child this coming summer and we have been very happy in this beautiful village until relatively recently. She is a teacher and we have such plans for it for a school for the younger children of which there are a few." He then looked down at the papers upon his desk with little enthusiasm.

"Then what has changed?" Jerome asked.

"Nothing as yet, but I fear it will soon enough. A major property on the edge of town is to be sold. It is an estate that holds the deeds for farms and town properties alike, and this lovely village, I feel, will not be valued by its new owner in the loving way it was by its past one. But, you catch me at a sensitive time. I really should not be discussing such business with you." He was watching Jerome closely.

Jerome leaned slightly forward. "But you can trust me because I am in the same profession. Is it breaking any law of confidentiality if you seek advice from a colleague?" He needed to gain Stanton's trust and quickly. He needed Stanton on side.

Geoffrey looked up at Jerome and smiled brightly. "Well, as you were listening so attentively to my conversation in the coffee house, I presume that you have some interest in the affair already and possibly some knowledge of it." He raised one eyebrow and both men laughed.

"Ah, Geoffrey, you were always observant. Very well, let us not play games with one another. I am glad to see that your mind is as razor sharp as it always was. Your assumption is quite correct. I have an interest in this business and I need to know more about what it is those rogues are up to. I have never seen or been a party to any of their business affairs. My concern is purely for the situation that the young lady you were discussing finds herself in. I can assure you that she did not run away, nor is she reckless, or damaged in reputation in any meaning of the word. She is safely returned to the home that has been hers to live in since her birth, no thanks to that sad excuse of a man, Bertram Munro. However, I fear that she has been kept away from the truth of her father's will and the details of her inheritance — should there be one. In so doing her cousin seeks to rid himself of her and take the land and everything else from under her feet. Why this man, Charles

Tripp, is so interested in the Hall I do not know. I am hoping that you do and will share some of the information with me so that together we can help her claim what is rightfully hers."

"I do not know why Tripp is involved with Munro either, officially, but I have made enquiries about him and have discovered that wherever he buys property or land he leaves a path of destruction behind him: a factory where houses once stood, or yards of industry where once green fields grew. The result, as I said, is the destruction of the small town or village they are linked to. He has done this twice that I know of. He purchases, provides the money for the work, and takes a hefty cut of the profits for a time and then moves on to his next target; all legal and all sickening if you are living in the path of his "progress". I apologise if I sound embittered, but there you have it. So, be plain, tell me, how can I help you?" Stanton sat back in his chair and watched keenly as Jerome explained.

"Is Parthena able, in any way, to block Bertram Munro from getting his hands on the estate?"

"Has she not shown you a copy of her father's will?" Stanton asked.

"She has not seen the will because she has been told that her father died intestate," Jerome answered, trying to conceal his anger.

"That is a lie! I left a copy for her with Bertram Munro. He insisted, as her father used to, that business is for men and that she should be protected from it. However, I stressed that she should be made aware of the contents as it was written with her father's intention that she know he left her cared for." Stanton was sitting up straight, eyes flashing with anger and indignation.

"But she was not protected from the consequences of the man who would do this to her, apparently. How much blind faith her father placed in blood and not in common sense. Did he even know this Bertram character?" Jerome asked.

"I think not, but then I also suspect that he hoped to live longer and find Parthena a suitor. I understand he had written to a friend in London, but his son was about to announce his engagement to another, so nothing came of it."

"So the very person who should have protected her cast her off," Jerome said.

"That is true. The only way she can have any ownership of the land is if she is married by the end of this month," Stanton explained and shrugged. "It is, as Bertram Munro said, impossible. Then she, or rather her husband, could make a direct claim to the total inheritance. But if she had been told the truth when the will was disclosed to Bertram they would have had six months or more for her to possibly find a suitor."

"Instead he planned a way of losing her or dishonouring her reputation to such an extent that marriage would not be possible. The bastard!" Jerome snapped.

"The one thing that was personally gifted to her along with an allowance of three hundred pounds per annum, so long as the estate exists, is the grandfather clock from the hallway, and this," Stanton said as he leaned into his drawer and pulled out a sealed letter. "This is part of the arrangements that are not mentioned in the will itself, which Mr Bertram Munro does not know about. You see, it is a letter and key, which was entrusted to me to give to Miss Munro in the event of her twenty-first birthday, if she was not wed and he, Mr Munro senior, had predeceased by that date. It is the only thing that her father did that may in some way protect her. However, if the estate does not exist as it has for the last few generations her allowance would cease anyway. She could be left almost destitute." Stanton shook his head in disgust.

"Do you know what it is for, and when will she be twenty-one?" Jerome asked.

"She was twenty-one last Wednesday, two days after she disappeared. I do not know what the key is for, but she may well recognise it."

"Then you must give it to her, without Bertram's presence or knowledge." Jerome sat forward, leaning on the desk.

"I agree, but you forget she is no longer here and that presents me with a slight logistical problem as well as a dilemma. When, if ever, do I tell her cousin about it?" Stanton raised both hands up in despair. "I believe in justice and want to help her, for it is obvious that there is something very wrong in this affair, yet without proof, and with the threat of them taking the legalities elsewhere, I am powerless to act."

"Mr Bertram Munro lied. Parthena did not run away, neither is she given to fits and tantrums and she certainly would not do something as reckless as he suggested. Let me explain what happened, and then we will find a way for you to see her so that you can deliver that envelope to her in person. Perhaps if you could call on her tomorrow at eleven we shall discover if she has a chance to extricate herself from the mess that has befallen her. I will make sure she is there at the Hall awaiting your arrival and that Mr Bertram Munro is not." Jerome was enraged, but he was not surprised, for he had met many an unscrupulous or greedy man in the course of his legal work, who thought little of the consequences of his actions on the dependant females in their charge.

"How and why would you do this for her if your paths only crossed briefly?" Geoffrey Stanton asked, after Jerome had filled him in on his and Parthena's journey so far.

"Because, as I have told you already, Geoffrey, I believe in seeing justice done. But, more than that, I believe I have quite fallen under Miss Munro's spell. I shall not return to my home until I have sorted this affair out to a satisfactory conclusion."

"Then you have my blessing and I will do what I can to aid you. But Tripp is a very powerful man and he could destroy me too, Jerome. I have a family to think about."

"You need not fear, Geoffrey. I will not see you or your reputation harmed in any way. If everything goes to plan, we all face a happier future. If Miss Munro turns down my offer, then I will offer you a position in my own firm. You would lose a village, but gain a more affluent career. Not perhaps what you wish, but it would secure a future for that growing family of yours." Jerome stood up.

"Very well." Stanton shook his hand. "You are quite a guardian angel to waifs and strays." He smiled. "You intend to propose to her, do you not?"

"I have only managed to save to a few wronged individuals who have happened across my path." Jerome shut off the memories of men's death screams from his recent past and cleared his throat. "And, yes, I intend to offer her the opportunity to become my wife and save her estate, but believe me, I am no one's guardian angel!"

"But you act when you can and no one can do more than that," Stanton said. "She would be an absolute fool to turn you down, Jerome."

"Then let us hope she is wise beyond her years." Jerome nodded and left, trying to bury his demons deep and focus upon his faerie of the night and his current mission to save a village from needless destruction.

Chapter 11

Bertram Munro burst into Leaham Hall with a purposeful stride which surprised Elsie Hubbart as she was about to take a warm drink of milk and honey up the stairs to Parthena.

"What is the meaning of this, Hubbart? Where are you going with that? I have told you before that you are not to be seen on the main stairs, in the hallway or anywhere that visitors may be disturbed by your presence — use the servants' corridors. This is your last warning!" Bertram barked his words out before Elsie had the chance to say anything in explanation.

"I was taking it, this drink…" She held the tray up as he glanced back at her, his face full of colour, "…upstairs, sir, for the young mistress … who returned to us today."

"Who returned? What nonsense do you speak, woman?" Bertram threw his coat down on the table and tossed his hat down also, but he and Elsie watched as the hat skidded across the table top and fell onto the floor at the other side of it.

"Hubbart!" he barked. "Pick that up!" The woman's hand began to shake as she held on to the tray, conscious that the warmed milk was beginning to spill. Her lips parted as if she was going to be bold enough to speak out, but she was to be saved from the repercussions that her vexed retort would have on him.

"Cousin, I am so glad that you have returned. I have so much to tell you." Parthena's voice drifted down from the upper landing. She was leaning over the banister, smiling.

"Parthena! Is that really you?" Bertram stood, gazing up, the colour draining from his face.

"Yes, cousin, who else would it be?" Parthena came down the stairs as gracefully as she could, laughing at his comment.

"You … you are returned to us?" Bertram took a step backwards and steadied himself against the edge of the hall table as Parthena walked calmly down the last few steps and stood before him.

"Well, where else would I have gone when I found myself unable to make the introduction you had arranged for me?" She laughed. "This is my home!"

"But you left intent on making a new life… You were adamant and…" Bertram was glancing awkwardly around at Elsie, his eyes darting from one woman to the other.

"Of course, with your letter in my bag and your clear instructions in my head, I had every faith that your arrangements would see me safely delivered into the company of your good friends. However, you were misinformed. You see, the people had moved on. There was no Major, wife or sons to meet me or at the address I was given. I discovered they had moved on months previously. I am afraid it was all a completely wasted trip. Enjoyable nonetheless. So, tell me, how are you finding Leaham Hall? The old place does have a certain charm about it, doesn't it, cousin?" Parthena's manner was deliberately as light as she could make it, though her whole being wanted to launch a tirade of questions at him as to how he could do such a callous thing to her when he already had the right to own her home.

Bertram fought to regain his composure. "But that is abominable! You must tell me what awful plight, my dear cousin, has befallen you. We must act quickly to repair your reputation and find somewhere peaceful where you can recover. Why you took off so wilfully and how you are returned to us so … how can it be, so safely as you profess?"

Parthena thought that Bertram was confused for a moment, perhaps in shock. Then she realised that he was trying to give off a sense of her fall to the servant.

"I mean, under the circumstances, the thought of what you have been through does not bear consideration." Bertram was rubbing his forehead with his handkerchief. "We must keep you away from prying eyes and gossip — no, a safe place, in peace and solitude. Come, we shall talk in my study," he said and gestured for her to follow him.

Parthena was aware that Elsie was listening to them with great interest and that Bertram was skewing the conversation to discredit her reputation further.

"Why nothing has befallen me, Cousin Bertram!" she said, her voice deliberately patronising. "Whatever are you thinking? My schooling was partially completed at a convent school in the same town — the Abbey School. Of course, you would have no way of knowing such details." She smiled as if a mystery had been effectively solved. Parthena remembered what Jerome had taught her, that to weave a convincing lie you merely embellished the truth on which it hung. "I merely asked the Mother Superior at the abbey for help and she gladly arranged my safe return. I was never in any peril, Cousin Bertram, of that you can be quite certain. Why, that would have been devastating, and I know you only had my best interests at heart when you arranged the position for me. No, I could not have been better looked after if it had all been planned that way. If you wish to write and thank her for her good care of me and donate to the abbey for her kindness I can give you the address; she is such an inspiring woman. So, you must tell me how things fare here. I understand there are to be changes made." She glanced around at Elsie who was looking from one cousin to the other, taking all in.

"We shall not gossip in the hall like servants, Parthena. Come into the morning room and we shall discuss this matter further. This venture of yours may have had some grave implications," Bertram said, keeping to his chosen theme, and then he turned his attention to Elsie. "Not a word of this to anyone, Hubbart, you hear!"

"No, sir," she said, as she made her way down the corridor and back to the servants' domain.

Parthena walked ahead of him. She heard Bertram bark another order out for them not to be disturbed. Parthena did not like the word, but the emotion that she felt towards the insufferable man who had gained a position of some authority over her could best be described as hatred.

Calmly, Parthena sat in the window seat and looked over to the marble-framed fireplace. A memory of it adorned with fresh leaves for the Christmas season made her swallow back her nostalgia for a time she could never recapture. Even if this home, by some miracle, became hers again, it would have to move forward. She would not live in a mausoleum dedicated to the past, no matter how much she missed it.

Bertram took his position before the fire, even though it was not lit. He held his hands behind his back as if it was still giving out warmth. His girth, she noticed, seemed to be growing as the weeks passed by.

"You have been on a pointless, yet perilous, journey of folly. Are you certain you escaped it … unharmed?" he asked, and watched her reaction closely.

She smiled back at him, innocence personified. "I do not know what you mean, Cousin Bertram. Why would the nuns want to hurt me in any way? In fact, it was a joy to see the place again. I loved the Abbey School and it had not changed much at all. The abbey itself is such a place of peace." She straightened her skirts as she spoke. She hated lying, but as she had decided she hated the man even more, she did it with great ease. "It gave me time to think about things here, and how we may have got off on the wrong footing. But as you are no doubt aware, I was grieving deeply for my poor father. I really do not know what possessed me to think of taking such a position, although I realise you were only trying to keep my mind occupied so that I did not grieve too deeply. Of course, I should stay here and help you. After all, some of the tenant families have been with the farms for generations and I should introduce you to them." She saw him pale further.

"You took the position, Parthena, because there are few options for you to consider, and staying here is not one of them. I assure you that…"

"But why? I apologise if I had seemed rude or upset by your arrival. It was just the emotions of my grief that overwhelmed me. So let us start afresh and you can tell me what plans you have for the future."

"No… No… No…"

Loud knocking at the door interrupted the flow of his words.

"Damnation! Who the hell can that be? If it's a tradesman I'll have his skin for coming to the front door. Your father was too soft with these people. They show no respect!" He stormed out of the room muttering under his breath.

Before Elsie could answer it, Bertram was at the door. He had dispensed with the services of Parthena's father's butler, Mr Kendal, as soon as he had been summoned to the estate. He was a man who trusted no one and who was paranoid about people getting close to him or his business affairs.

Bertram flung the door open wide and was ready to blast the unsuspecting figure who he found at the other side of it with his outrage, when he found a well-dressed gentleman standing innocently on his doorstep. The man's tall, athletic frame accentuated by his high hat and fashionably cut coat struck of money and position, and stopped Bertram from ranting at him.

"Yes? Good day, sir?" Bertram tried to regain his composure.

Jerome looked at the portly figure in front of him. "Is the master of the house in, I would like to call upon him?" he asked.

Bertram glared at the man. He was at the point of bursting with indignation; could he be undermined any further, he wondered, by women or circumstances? Now a stranger of some wealth presumed him to be the blasted butler — it was more than enough to send him into a turn!

Jerome suppressed a smile. Bertram breathed in unnaturally deeply and then exhaled slowly. Jerome watched him as if he were acting in slow motion. Good heavens, he thought, the man is going to have a fit! If it turned out to be more than a moment of anxiety or controlled rage then Parthena's problems may be solved another way. Unfortunately, as Jerome suspected, Bertram regained his composure.

"I am he! Not the butler, sir, but the owner of this grand estate!" Bertram snapped out his words and in that moment Jerome knew the man was completely wrong-footed. This was a meeting he was going to enjoy.

Chapter 12

"My greatest apologies, sir," Jerome said, lifting his hat and allowing his dark hair to rest freely upon the collar of his coat. He removed his hand from his pocket and offered Bertram his card.

Bertram took it as he regained his temper and stared at the address in The Inns of Court, London. He swallowed and then smiled. "My dear sir, to what do I owe this pleasure? You seem to have caught me slightly off-guard — my butler will have a firm word in his ear I can assure you. Please, please, come in." Bertram stepped back and shouted, "Hubbart! Hubbart!"

Jerome expected the chastened butler to emerge forlorn, but instead a woman appeared from the door that obviously led to the hidden servants' corridor. She seemed vexed.

"Yes, Mr Munro…" She stopped and took a moment to look at Jerome. "Oh! Let me take your coat, sir," she said and busied herself around Jerome.

"I shall not be my own footman!" Bertram snapped.

Jerome saw the piercing glare as the woman glanced up at Bertram. This woman was holding back a tirade and her flushed cheeks betrayed her even if her mouth did not, but Bertram was oblivious to her feelings as he smiled at Jerome.

"Arrange for a tray to be sent to my study," Bertram ordered. He waved the woman away. Jerome saw her grip tighten when Bertram walked ahead of her. Jerome realised that this man had no idea how to treat anyone, servant or not.

"Now, tell me, to what do I owe this visit, sir?" His manner was pleasant enough until he heard Jerome's startling reply.

"I bumped into an old friend of mine, Mr Charles Tripp. I believe you and he are well acquainted…"

"Why, yes, very…"

"…and he suggested that I called upon you if I were in the vicinity." Jerome raised his brows. "Is this a good time, or would you prefer that I return at a later hour…?" Jerome let his voice drift off as Bertram shrugged, smiled and then gestured with an overdramatic sweep of his arm that he should follow him. Bertram continued to walk ahead towards a door that Jerome presumed was the study but Jerome stopped and stepped back as Parthena appeared in the doorway opposite. Jerome looked at her and winked. She was even more beautiful when dressed in her normal finery; those delightful eyes so obviously pleased to see him. Her manner was relaxed in her natural surroundings and it suited her well, despite the chaos that surrounded her reappearance here.

Parthena quickly walked over to Jerome as she had that first night. It was only a short time ago, yet she had quite innocently woven her magic upon him. How much knowledge he had of her, her body, her secrets and her plight, and how much more he would love to know. If his mother had introduced him to a daughter of her society friends the dating ritual would have played itself out and they would be wed after months of polite visitations, and yet they still might be as strangers to each other on their wedding night. Before the wars he would have been happy with that, it would have been what he would have expected. Anything more would have been considered inappropriate, but not now. Jerome now understood the value of life, passion and hope. Time went too quickly for some. He no longer cared about trinkets and trivia.

Considering Parthena, he would know the real woman, the true self that was normally hidden behind a polite and shallow veneer. A woman who was strong enough in mind and body to do what was needed to survive. To cross an open moor on her own! There was a woman who stood at one with nature and he was even surer that she was the woman he sought; his life's partner, his soulmate.

Bertram coughed. He had been saying something to Jerome as he walked into the study's doorway, presuming Jerome would follow him. Jerome had only a moment to pass on his message to Parthena, so he quickly mouthed to her, "Be ready at eleven o'clock tomorrow morning."

Bertram turned and saw Jerome looking back at Parthena. He must have realised she had caught his attention and moved to stand between them. "Please let me introduce you to my ward, Miss Parthena Munro, my cousin, sir." Bertram looked at her as if she were a naughty, intrusive child.

"I am pleased to meet you, miss." Jerome saw her eyes glint with humour, even if she kept a polite expression of indifference upon those sweet lips.

"This gentleman has come to talk to me from his offices in London, on legal business. We will finish our discussion later, Parthena. Now do run along, my dear, you must have some sewing to do," Bertram instructed and Jerome saw a distinct flash of anger cross her eyes, but he raised an eyebrow and she took the hint.

"Of course, cousin." She then looked directly at Jerome and nodded slightly. "Until later, Bertram and Mr...?"

"Mr Jerome Fender at your service, miss," he said, and bowed slightly. He felt the faintest hint of a grin beginning to form across his face and decided that the two of them had played out this scene long enough. He gestured toward the man's study. "Should we?" he asked.

"Of course, Mr Fender," Bertram said, and led him into the room, closing the door tightly behind them. The brief discussion of the weather and the state of the older roads ended once a tray was in place and Elsie had, like Parthena, disappeared from their presence.

"So, please tell me why my dear friend Charles has requested you visit me here. Is this in connection with Stanton and our business dealings?" Bertram was oblivious to subtlety, that was obvious to Jerome.

Jerome crossed his legs and leaned back casually in the fireside chair. For his plan to work he needed two things to happen: firstly to convince this worm of a man that he was as incorrigible as Bertram was himself, and secondly, to find out if Parthena was as willing to save her village as he desired to have her as his wife.

"I am of the understanding that you and Charles are soon to exchange papers on this Hall."

Bertram folded his arms across his girth and nodded.

"And that by the end of the month all must be arranged and the deeds handed over," Jerome began confidently. "The fate of the village sealed, as it were."

"Yes, it is so. We have a gentleman's agreement, sir." Bertram stood up straight. "Tell me, sir, if you wish to bid for it, for I must inform you that the land attached to this estate includes many farms, some workshops, forestry and also the river rights. There is an old tin mine and un-mined seams of copper. The river alone has excellent trout. So, in all, you would need a large sum to outbid Charles for it, if that is your intention. Then there is the damage it would do to our friendship if I let Charles down — that would also cost me dearly." Bertram blinked as he stared hopefully at Jerome.

Jerome stared back at Bertram for a moment. He resisted the urge to punch his supercilious face.

"However…" Bertram continued, "I am a fair man and Charles would understand, as he often reminds me that he is a man of business and not sentiment." Bertram's eyes were fixed on Jerome's as he studied his visitor for a reaction.

Jerome had bluffed far stronger opponents and wiser enemies than this cad, so he continued calmly, "Indeed, which is precisely why I am not making a bid for the estate." He wished that he had enough reserves separate to his own family estate to buy everything, for here he had seen a peaceful, functioning community that had so much more potential if the people were allowed to look after their land themselves.

In order to gain the opportunity to see Parthena privately he had to have Bertram on side. Jerome must persuade this pitiful creature that he was in the pay of Charles Tripp in some way and would remove Parthena from their path, temporarily or permanently. Jerome was to become a rogue to save the day.

"No, it is not the land I want, sir, as my Kent estate takes up so much of my time when I am not in Pall Mall." He saw Bertram's eyes light up. "It is the young lady who interests me, especially after setting eyes upon her again just now in all her finery. Ah those eyes! Are they not special? Have you rarely seen such gems shining out of a young maid's face."

"What? Eyes… I've never noticed anything special about her eyes, other than she has two…" Bertram muttered and laughed at his own weak humour.

"I understood from Charles that she had vanished from your care, and yet I realised, when I met him at The Turn Pike Inn to discuss own business, that the lady I had seen alight from the coach asking for transport to Leaham Hall was in fact your missing cousin." He raised his two hands palms up in a gesture to stress what a find he had made.

Bertram jumped slightly. "I do not follow." Bertram was becoming agitated again. "What would Charles be discussing Miss Munro's unenviable situation with you for, sir? I assure you if you are considering a rushed engagement, or some sort of land grab, then I have to tell you that, as her legal guardian I would refuse such a brazen act outright. You may want more of her than her eyes, but you will not even have a hair of her obnoxious head!" His words were interrupted when Jerome burst forth with loud guffaws of laughter.

Jerome calmed himself and coughed as if to clear his throat. "My very good man, you jump to the wrong conclusion, I can assure you! How low you think of me and my reputation if you would even consider such a plan. Despite the fact that I would be breaking the law of bigamy, as my own dear wife would hardly agree to move over to make room for the girl, the idea that I would risk my career on hitching myself to such a wayward, flighty creature as Charles described to me is very amusing." He shook his head. "I have not laughed so heartily in a long time. I do not doubt she has some good breeding, but you are talking about a wench that will up and run away at the first sign of things not going her way. No, that is not what I meant at all."

"Oh, forgive me. I obviously misunderstood." Bertram looked greatly relieved, but was quite flustered by the turn of events. He certainly did not understand what Jerome was about, but by his keen expression it was obvious that he wanted to know more. "You see I thought she, with those "eyes", may have somehow bewitched your better nature, sir. My apologies." He leaned forward slightly. "So what did you mean?"

"No, sir, I am not so easily taken in. I simply meant that I can see a way to remove her and lose her for you without any chance of her returning, quite legitimately and without question." He winked at Bertram. Perhaps his gesture was a bit overdone, he thought, but this man would not take subtle hints so a barge pole would have to do. "If that would help?" Jerome added, and leaned forward interlacing the fingers of his hands in front of him as he did so. "Are you interested, for although I would gain entertainment from this distraction, I will not stay and repeat my offer if you are not. As I explained, I have a very high reputation to uphold."

Jerome watched the man take the bait. He deliberately shifted in his chair as if considering arising and leaving.

"But how would you do this, and why?" Bertram was now sitting on the edge of the chair he had pulled up opposite Jerome, leaning and listening with intensity to Jerome's words.

Jerome deliberately leered at him. He had the man in the palm of his hand. "Very simply, I would have entertainment with her and I would by helping you secure the money for the estate I would be helping release a debt I have to Charles."

"This is indeed fortuitous for all," Bertram said, and clasped his hands together.

Jerome felt his anger rising. This man would be no better than the slavers who had made a living from the misery of others' lives.

"Very well, how will you do this?" Bertram whispered. "You can tell me the detail and I will not breathe a word." His eyes widened like two round coat buttons.

"I will dazzle her with promises. I mean to invite her to London to be a companion to my dear young sister, Eleanor, for the Season and offer her the delights and fashions that the Season requires. If all goes well we will tell her that she will have a permanent position. And when my sister must attend finishing school in Paris, she may find herself a husband, and we will help with introductions to suitable suitors. How easy it will be to dazzle and bemuse her young woman's mind." He smiled, hating the rogue he was portraying, yet after years at war, a mere deception to a greedy fool was really neither here nor there on the scale of his 'sins'. Besides, this was in a very good cause. Bertram's sins, he suspected, were many and deep.

"And will you do all this for her?" Bertram looked incredulously at him. "She hardly deserves such treatment."

"No, of course not, man!" Jerome laughed. "Why on earth would I? She would completely discredit me in front of my peers. But she will believe all, for she is an impressionable wench, is she not?"

Bertram slowly nodded and so Jerome continued, for the man needed a plan spelling out to him. "Therefore, when she willingly steps into my carriage, believing this to be so, she will be filled with enthusiasm for an adventure in a very different and exciting world. You do not need to know any more details about what befalls her. I will send word that she has run off with some young dandy who turned her head, if you wish to know anything, but a woman with such looks is always in demand in London, believe me." He winked at Bertram who was so eager to believe his problems had been solved that he would apparently agree to any subterfuge Jerome offered.

If Jerome could arrest Bertram then and there for his part in this make-believe scenario he would. He would like to save Parthena, but in the process see Bertram fall. He wondered if Stanton had made enquiries into Bertram's estate or affairs.

Bertram smiled. "I do not need to know any more. I shall leave it all to your judgement. She will never return here you say? You are absolutely certain of this? Because it has happened once already and I cannot risk another error of judgement — the clock is ticking!"

"Not a chance of it. She will most likely end up on foreign shores — those blue eyes you see — she will be in such demand," Jerome answered and looked into the flames of the small fire. He wondered if justice would be done beyond this life if Hell's fire really existed and if Bertram was to become acquainted with it, for the man deserved nothing less.

"Yes, yes I see!" Bertram said, a note of excitement making his voice rise.

His enthusiasm sickened Jerome, but he did not show his disdain.

"Good! May I suggest I dine with you tonight and we can persuade Miss Parthena that her future would be best served by taking me up on my offer?" Jerome tilted his head innocently on one side.

"Yes, yes of course. Do you wish to stay the night?" Bertram asked, apparently quite taken by his cunning new friend.

"I am afraid I cannot, for I have a room in the town, but perhaps you could meet me in the coffee shop tomorrow, say at a half past the hour of ten, and we can run through the details of when I should leave with her. That is, if she is willing to go along with my ruse. She must leave here happily, even if her happiness will not endure once in the city. I have my reputation to consider as I have already said, and will not have it sullied," Jerome said and smiled.

"No, you must not raise any suspicion at all. We shall fill her head with promises of jewels, finery, dances."

"Good man!" Jerome said and patted his shoulder.

"Excellent idea. I will arrange for dinner then. Do you wish to meet her now? Soften her up a little." Bertram winked at him.

"Excellent notion! Perhaps she could show me the garden and the path by the river. I understand from Charles the fishing here is also excellent. Best to enjoy it whilst you still can."

"I am not a sporting man, Mr Fender, my gifts are better suited to a boardroom."

Jerome could not believe how easily Bertram had fallen into his wild plan. Jerome knew that if he wished he could indeed follow through and do this to Parthena, take her and sell her into a scandalous trade and her own cousin would let it be so. It was said that love was blind, but greed was a much stronger blindfold to an evil man's senses, it appeared.

"Yes, give me a moment and I will ask her to make herself ready for a stroll around the open gardens," Bertram said. He scuttled from his study, which gave Jerome a chance to look around. He saw the large folder upon the desk and had a quick glimpse inside. He had seen enough plans and drawings to quickly ascertain that Charles Tripp was not interested in fishing, but the fast flow of the river and the position of the estate gave it a favourable aspect for the building of a mill. More than one building was planned, though; there was a manufactory also. Stanton was correct. These plans would destroy the heart of the village. They would certainly destroy the heart of his friend Stanton — his dream of a haven to raise his family in would be blown away with the leaves of autumn.

Would Parthena marry him to save the home and the livelihoods of the estate workers? Persuading Bertram to trick her was the easy part, but persuading Parthena to wed him for the good of the village, or to please his heart's desire was a mountainous task. She had no time to think about it and neither had he. Jerome could be seen as a prospector who had learned the truth of the will and wished to also steal her beauty and her birthright, or simply an opportunist, but would she see that he genuinely adored her? It would have to involve a great deal of trust placed in him. He closed the file and sat back down in the chair, awaiting Bertram's return. He did not want to think on it anymore. If he could have Parthena he would be a contented man.

Bertram blustered in, shaking his head. "Women! I shall never understand them and am pleased to say that thus far I have escaped their grasp. I have no wish to have one pester me day and night. However, I will need an heir for my new estate soon enough." He shrugged.

"Are you staying on here then?" Jerome asked, confused for a moment.

"No, no, not this one. This estate is too provincial, Mother would never settle to it! No, with the proceeds from the sale of this I have plans to buy a larger property in Kent. Mother has always been desirous of land near Hythe; perhaps we will be neighbours in future. So, once the funds of this one are through I can make the dear lady's dream come true and then will be the time to marry and think of an heir to carry on the Munro name."

He did not look happy at the prospect.

"You are planning quite an adventure yourself it seems," Jerome remarked.

"Yes, quite. Mother will choose a wife for me. I prefer a timid soul. Not too fancy and certainly not one who craves soirées and gems. Mother will see to her education in the finer points of being a landed gentleman's wife," he explained. "I believe she has already begun the search. Mother is such a lady of taste it will be a fine maid who she settles upon." A smile momentarily spread across Bertram's rotund face.

Parthena knocked on the door of the study.

"Ah, there you are. Could you show Mr Munro around the grounds, my dear?"

Parthena looked taken aback. "Are you not joining us, Bertram?"

"I shall watch you from the window, but I fear my gout plays up again and I must save myself for dinner."

"Very well," Parthena answered. If she was trying to look less than enthusiastic, Jerome thought she was doing an excellent job of it.

"Thank you, Miss Munro." Jerome stood up. "I should like to enjoy the gardens and, as for the fishing, I hear it is excellent." He smiled and addressed Bertram. "Then I shall return to the village and arrange for the coach."

"The coach?" Parthena repeated, as they walked to the main door.

"Yes, I intend to return to London for the Season. My sister is so looking forward to it." He was walking alongside Parthena and she was paying him a deal of attention, which he hoped would impress Bertram who was following on behind, at least to the threshold of the Hall. "Tell me, Miss Munro, have you seen Pall Mall or the gardens at Vauxhall? They are absolutely divine and I am certain you would adore them."

"Why no, Mr Fender, I have not. Tell me, is there not unrest in London about the price of corn?" she asked and noted the surprise on both men's faces.

"My dear girl, what talk is that for a young lady to greet a guest," Bertram admonished and then faced Jerome. "I apologise. Perhaps you will need to advise Parthena as to what is appropriate conversation for the dinner table from a young woman's lips and what is not!"

"It is fine, Bertram. I can assure you, Miss Munro, I would not take you into a dangerous situation. You are indeed lucky here that you do not rely on corn for the estate and have a good number of sheep and cattle too. There were some protests around Westminster but they have long since been quelled," Jerome said and half smiled at her.

"Would you care to tell me about them as we walk?" she asked, as she started down the steps to the path that skirted around the old building to the main gardens, taking great care not to stand too close to him.

"Yes, of course, I will tell you of the delights you can find in London and leave the politics to the tedium of men," Jerome said, and waited a moment before turning to Bertram and whispering to him, "By the end of this week, you shall say goodbye to your cousin for good and she you."

Bertram slapped him on his back and chuckled. "Good man," he replied, before shutting the door on them without a glance back for Parthena's safety.

Chapter 13

Parthena was surprised by Bertram's request that she walk with Jerome alone around the grounds. If Jerome had not whispered to her in the hallway previously, she would have doubted where his loyalty lay, as he had seemed very eager to engage in conversation with Bertram. He played his role, whatever it was, with complete and convincing confidence.

"So tell me, Mr Fender, what guise do you appear in today, using your own name, but having Bertram's agreement to our meeting — and in relative privacy?" She stopped at a rose and pointed to it as though discussing its colour or scent. "You seem to have captivated him in some way."

"Simply this, Thena. I have come to him as myself, offering him my help in solving a problem that I have recently become aware of by a man who I am claiming to be a close acquaintance." He smiled politely at her as they walked and talked.

"What is that?" she asked.

"Why, you, of course. I overheard him talking in the coffee house in the village and have used my position to infer that I know his business partner and am a party to the knowledge that you stand in the way of him and their intentions."

"That is very bold of you. What if the business partner should visit?"

"He will not do that, yet. Since arriving here, I have seen the drawings in Bertram's study and they do indeed paint a dark future for this beautiful place." He pointed at a tree as they passed it and she nodded, all to good innocent effect as Bertram looked unwittingly on from the Hall. "It appears it is to be completely destroyed in the guise of progress, as a mill is to be built and the village is to be crammed with new but cheaply-made housing."

"I have too. I am beside myself with worry, as I cannot see how to stop this from happening. He will destroy everything for the people who have lived and worked here their whole lives. The village and the land will be changed forever. It distresses me as there seems to be nothing I can do about it, Jerome," she said, and looked up at him. "I owe you so much already, and I doubt I can ever repay you, but is there any way you can help me to prevent him in his this? I fear that the destruction he plans may bring back a plague like the one that nearly destroyed this place centuries ago. You are a man of the law — is there any hope?" She had to turn away from the Hall to regain her composure. Her words were driven by the heat of passion that she felt for her home and by the desperate loneliness she had felt since her father died.

"That is why I am here, Thena. There may be a way, but it will involve great sacrifice and even greater trust. I met an old colleague of mine, a man who was at the Inns when I was there," Jerome explained.

Parthena looked at him and repeated, "The inns, what inns? Did he see us?" Her mind reeled at the thought that someone in the village knew that she had spent a night with Jerome.

"Not that kind of inn. The Inns of Court, Lincoln's Inn… We were in chancery together."

"Oh," she said, "I see."

"Come, walk and talk with me further. We must not arouse his suspicion. Bertram must believe I am a cad and that you are being duped." They walked along with a foot or so between them so that they did not touch, even by accident. "Mr Stanton trained where I did, at the same law school. He is your family's legal representative and speaks well of your father and the village. He has kept a gift for you from your father — a key, and I believe a letter for your twenty-first birthday, to be given to you with the grandfather clock he also left you. Stanton did not tell Bertram of this, as it was for you only. Not even when you disappeared did he say a word. He is an honourable man. Bertram would have had him believe you had run away, Parthena. I am sorry and do not mean to frighten you further but your cousin is wicked. If I could lock him up for his intentions I would have done, but he has not done anything yet that could prove his guilt in court. Therefore, I need you to stay strong, alert and play out the roles I have invented for us both." Jerome was watching her closely for her reaction; she could tell he was deeply concerned by whatever Bertram and he had discussed.

"He seeks to destroy my reputation as he failed to destroy me outright. I have been thinking long and hard on this. Any man who could send a woman to a place where she would be left desolate is of low character and immoral intent. So, I realise that my return here has placed me in a difficult and possibly dangerous situation. I do not know, Jerome, what he is capable of. He may send me to a convent next! If I was given the choice between being thrown out or sent into their care, how could I refuse? I am frightened. If I cross him, if he realises that I … that we are in collusion, we could both be in peril. I am beginning to wonder just how far he will go. Will he stop at nothing to gain his rights to this land and rid himself of any obligation for my care?"

Jerome clenched his fists and they had to walk a few paces in order not to fulfil the desire in both of their eyes to hold hands, to unite in a common cause, or to simply find solace in the embrace of another human being.

Parthena looked to the river. "I knew Father must have left his affairs in order!" she said, and was filled with a rush of emotion. Then added, "I would never just up and run away!" She was appalled at how devious her cousin had proved to be. What must Jerome be thinking of her and her small, but seemingly corrupt, family? She hoped that he did not believe that it ran in her bloodline, this evil spirit, and that was why she had stolen from him. "Oh, please, dear God, let that message reveal some light that can obliterate Bertram's wicked shadow over us," she said, and then remembered to point at a bird flying low over the water as they continued. Subterfuge seemed to be her friend at present, but it was hard to keep up the pretence when she was so worried and angry.

"Calm yourself, Thena, for there is a way." Jerome, too, stopped a moment to admire the view.

Parthena could not help but smile.

"What amuses you so?" Jerome asked.

"My dear father has left me time." She looked up at the sun. "That clock represents the words of wisdom that he shared with me and reminds me of how precious our time with loved ones is." Then she saddened. "If only he had foreseen this mess and the nature of my cousin... If only I had loved ones left to care for me or me them... If only..."

"Oh, Thena, he has left you precious little time. The will clearly leaves the estate to your cousin. The legacy of the land applies to it being kept as it is, if inherited by the direct line. The wording is not specific enough, and although it stipulates what happens if it is passed from father to son, or son-in-law, because it was poorly prepared, the codicil of the land being kept as is does not transfer once the original line is side-stepped to another relative, like Bertram."

Jerome was trying to make this simple for Parthena to understand, she knew that, but the unfairness of it all galled her. "If what you say is true, Bertram has won. This charade is pointless, my return is pointless. I should have just stayed in the abbey and never taken your coin. For that I am truly sorry and it does not run in the blood…"

"What does not?" He looked at her most perplexed.

"The badness that would drive a person to take what was not theirs." She stared at him and he her.

"I never thought it was. I have seen desperate people and know we all fall short when our limits are pushed. War does that to a person. Poverty does that and, in some wretched people, greed does that."

"You are too kind. I cannot stop this sale. I and this community will fall to the chimneys of progress." She stared back at the house, but Jerome coughed and continued walking to bring her back to their situation and break through her anger. "When I think of what will become of the village…"

They stopped walking along the banks of the river. Jerome glared down at the water as if trying to see the fish through its depth.

"There is a way that you can save all of this, Thena, but it requires a great sacrifice on your part, along with a willingness to trust me again." Jerome was staring at her. It seemed as if he was trying to tell her something without using words, willing her to understand … but what? Parthena saw his face betray how serious he was about what he was going to say to her. She could tell by the way his features moved that he was trying to find the words he wanted, to explain to her as simply and effectively as possible what it was he had discovered. She wanted to shake him and ask him to spit his words out if necessary — she had to know if there was a way, she would take it, whatever the cost. How difficult could it be for a man of law to express his thoughts, she wondered, but then his words came back to her... 'Or son-in-law', and then she swallowed. Was he really thinking of stepping in to rescue her again? Surely a man like Jerome Fender already had a wife. But then he had been at war and war is a destroyer of the normal order of life. Or had he someone else in mind? Someone he knew or would pay for the convenience of marrying her in name only? She swallowed.

They walked along the river path a way, but stayed within view of the house as they were both aware that they were being watched keenly by Bertram as he stood in the long window of the morning room.

"Tell me before I burst, Jerome!" she said, under her breath.

Finally he spoke. "Thena, we have been thrown together in the most unlikely way, and yet I believe fate has had its hand in this. To stop Bertram and save your village you need to be married by the end of this month and a claim submitted to Stanton straight away. That is it in a nutshell." He faced her.

"It is impossible..." she began, thinking how short a time that was. Was he going to suggest they pay someone to quickly marry her? He could not be proposing himself ... surely.

"Hear me out, Thena, I do not wish to shock you... I know this is all very sudden and must seem incredulous to you, but he did not give you a chance to find a suitor, as he held the detail of the will's contents from your sight and knowledge for the past half year."

She shook her head, anger tasting like bile. "He has known all that time, and I have been treated like a mute child!"

Jerome nodded. Then he found his voice and his words flowed like a fast river. "That is the truth of it. If you wish to save your beautiful surroundings and look after the tenants' interest you must wed quickly. Unless you know someone you would prefer, then I can offer you the place of a wife. I have talked to Stanton and it can be done." He cleared his throat and watched her. "You can save yourself and all of this, if you will say yes."

"No!" The word came out awkwardly and quickly.

Jerome's head jolted back as if she had slapped his cheek with sudden unexpected force. "Then there is no more to be said or done. Your fate and that of your tenants and the village is sealed, barring a miracle of conscience striking Bertram or Tripp. Pardon my cynicism, but I do not believe in them. I have seen too much death in this world to believe in the goodness of human nature in such men." He began to turn away from her.

"Jerome, stop, please. You misunderstand what I mean. I think, I know what you imply, but it is impossible because the banns need weeks to be read out and… It is simply too late. We cannot do this in time. I do not know if you are offering yourself up as a sacrificial lamb, or Mr Stanton as a legal arrangement: either way, it is simply not possible."

"That is true, if you wed in church, in England, Thena, but there is another, more daring way. It involves a dash up country in a carriage, or by sea. It is a long journey. Have you heard of elopement to a place called Gretna Green? If we can cross the border then…" Jerome looked at her and smiled. "Scottish laws are very different to ours."

"How would I get away and why would you suggest that I marry you? I realise that you do not know me, let alone love me, or are you proposing on behalf of Mr Stanton? Is this a business arrangement?" She tried to make light of the situation, but as she saw movement behind the window back at the house Parthena realised their conversation had become so absorbing that Jerome's ruse was falling flat. She began walking forward again and was trying hard not to change the way she stepped out as they strolled purposefully along.

"No, not Stanton. He already has a wife." Jerome stepped alongside her again. "It is me who is proposing to you, Thena. I would be delighted if you would agree to be my wife. Therefore, I am suggesting that you and I go to Scotland and get a hasty marriage licence and return as quickly as possible to stop him, save your village and…" He looked away, momentarily pointed to some imagined point of interest, and then looked back at her. "Then you can really be my wife in every sense of the word, if you so wish to be, for I would like that very much."

Parthena stopped and stared at him, her eyes fixed on his and she could tell that he meant every word of it, Bertram momentarily forgotten. He would do this for her? "I do not think you have tried to see this clearly, Jerome. You are recently returned from war, you are still being a hero when here you can be whatever you want to be. You do not need to answer to anyone. You are a man of position and some wealth, therefore you do not need to give your freedom up so easily," she said, but he laughed.

"You have not met my mother, yet," he winked at her, "but you shall. Trust me, Thena. I know what I want and in having it I can help you. Do not think of me as a hero. In this, I have self-interest … you."

Parthena was trying to be confident in her manner, but she was taken aback. Why would he even consider her. Unless, of course, seeing the land, the estate, the inheritance has swayed his mind. He was, after all, a very astute man who was used to making verdicts based upon calculative facts. He did not have to be a mathematician to realise her husband stood to inherit a substantial sum. "True, you would honourably save the village, and me, but what then? You would have saddled yourself with a wife. Someone you hardly know, and there are a lot of problems here, as there are tenants and land rights and farmland to manage. Do you know anything about sheep? You are a barrister and you need to be at your Inns. Then there is your mother." She looked at him, he was smiling still. Did it not matter to him that this would be a loveless arrangement? Did he not realise that she was not prepared to play out the role of 'wife' in its entirety — yet? But she would agree to this rash act of wedding him because she would not lose the estate to Bertram's mill plan.

"I find you beautiful, beguiling and I would be happy for us to really get to know each other, but that part is up to you. I have been at war. I cannot deny that I am not the same arrogant man that first left these shores. I have grown and am a better one. I know now what I want from life and would relish the opportunity to learn everything about the land and farming … honestly." He shrugged. "All else can wait."

"How would this be done?" Parthena asked. She was still trying to think through his words. Did he mean he would not force her into a relationship and that he really would wait for her to be ready?

"How we would do this is simple. I am acting like a total rogue for the benefit of your cousin. Do not look shocked as I explain the depth to which Bertram will go to rid himself of you. I have offered to remove you to London. You need to look excited, Thena, as if I am selling you the dream of attending balls and being dressed in such finery that no head will be left unturned as you enter the assembly rooms. I am supposed to be dazzling you with the prospect of a chance to see Society in all its glory as part of this dream, and promise you that you will attend the finest events as companion to my fictitious younger sister, Eleanor, who is lonely." He waved a hand in the air as if describing something grand.

She smiled at his dramatic gesture but laughed anxiously more than excitedly. Could she trust Jerome? She knew so little about him and yet he knew all her darkest secrets. Could he be so genuine, so lovely, handsome and kind that he would truly forfeit his freedom for her? He could then legally sell everything from under her if he so wished. Then his words sank in. "What precisely was to happen to me in London that would prevent me from returning?" Her now vexed look had no pretence of joy and excitement about it.

"You would be virtually sold on to the highest bidder, foreign or not, and your freedom lost to you in a dirty trade that sadly does exist."

Parthena gasped and she quickly turned her back to Jerome and the Hall.

He kept talking to her. "But that was all lies for, although I dealt with a man who had been involved in this White Slave Trade and I sent him down for a long spell from which he may never return to harm another soul, I have no such contacts. I was weaving him a fantasy and he chose to believe it."

"He is the very devil himself!" Parthena snapped her words out. Her pace increased.

"No, not quite, but certainly one of his followers, although, fortunately for us, not so bright." Jerome caught up with her. "Thena, slow down, smile, laugh, out-play the man at his own game."

She stopped, turned and laughed, openly looking 'joyful' before bitterly saying, "He is devious, though, and we will have to be very careful; this could endanger not only the estate but our lives." She walked on, her mind spinning.

"Yes, you are correct and we have little time left, Thena. I am to dine here tonight and you must be full of enthusiasm to meet my sister and prepare to leave your home in my carriage, as if without a thought of looking back at this place. If you play this right and receive Stanton tomorrow morning, I will keep Bertram busy in the village, and then within two days you leave this place with me. But instead of heading south to my London residence, we head north at speed to Scotland, and in that way we can stop the blackguard." His words were filled with enthusiasm. "Today is the fourth day, we have just over three weeks to go, marry, return and claim the inheritance."

"Are you certain about all of this? Can it be done? You will not be free to marry if you find your true love, Jerome. Unless we divorce soon afterwards. Is that your plan? Can we, and then leave the estate to me to run?" she asked.

He laughed and shook his head. "Take heart, I have money and property, I do not need to take advantage of your situation, but I can see why you love this place and I would promise to protect it for generations to come from the likes of Tripp." He looked down at her with a great deal of concern in his eyes. "Thena, I know it is a very difficult decision for you to make, but if you do not do this I have no great vision of a happy future for you, and the village tenancies will be lost. Bertram, I believe, would wish you harm — he wants you gone from his path. If I could arrest him for what he would like to do, then I would, and he would be hanged, but he has not committed the act, yet, and I would be a broken man if I came so near to saving you, and lost the chance." He lifted a hand as if he was going to place it around her so she quickly moved away as that would look very suspect. "Besides, how can I arrest a man for wanting to be a part of a wicked scheme that I alone created. No, we have to do this with the law on our side."

"Jerome, next you will be declaring that you love me already…" It was her turn to look away and laugh, but his voice stopped her. He had ignored her question about getting a divorce.

"Would that be so unpalatable?" he asked, but walked on, not waiting for her to respond.

In truth she could not know, for his words were such a surprise to her. He was either a very sensitive and genuine person, despite his rank and profession, or an extremely good actor — but then legal men had to be so, she pondered. Either way, she was trapped by Bertram, or willingly agreed to be trapped by marriage and risk her trust on two men, Fender and Stanton; one had self-interest at heart in the village, and was friends with the other. She sighed. Why could she not have been born the son her father had so wanted?

Parthena caught up with Jerome and smiled brightly as they returned to the Hall. "Very well, if you are willing and sincere, then let our adventure continue, Mr Fender, and use whatever power you can to protect my villagers, my home and my heart, and destroy the vermin that has taken up residence within it. I will agree to your plan." She did not look for his response or wait for his reply. She boldly stepped back into the Hall as was expected of her, trying to stifle the urge to take one of her father's pistols and challenge Bertram to a duel — man to woman. She knew she could take him on, but had no wish to be hanged for murder.

"You enjoyed your walk, Parthena?" Bertram greeted her, eyebrows raised almost to comedic effect on his round face.

"Very much so, cousin. I have much to tell you," she said. "Mr. Fender has a sister of my own age, did you know? Her name is Eleanor and she is a delicate lady…"

"Oh, no, I did not. What a happy coincidence." Bertram nodded at Jerome as he entered. "You should meet her."

"Perhaps we could invite her to stay. The country air might do her some good," Parthena offered and saw Bertram's face flush.

"No!" He barked out the word.

"Why ever not?" she asked, enjoying the look of horror on the man's face as his plan seemed to be backfiring.

"She would never cope with the journey, Miss Munro," Jerome said. "Coaches shake you to the very bone," he added. "The roads are not very good in these parts. I think, as we discussed outside, it would be much better if you accompanied me back to London…"

Bertram coughed. "Yes, yes, exactly. Mr Fender will join us for dinner and we shall discuss this more then."

"Very well, Bertram," Parthena responded and passed by the grandfather clock. She smiled. Bertram's reign was about to come to an abrupt end. One way or another they would eject him. Then he could return to his mother and tell her that he had lost the inheritance he would have abused so ill.

Parthena was about to call Elsie to help her pack when she realised that was one way of setting tongues wagging again. She returned to her room alone to repack for a very different journey. Sitting on the edge of the bed she thought carefully about the minimum of garments that she would need if she was to return here. Two dresses and travel clothes, undergarments, night wear… One thought made her stop momentarily above all others — it would be her wedding. She should feel something — excitement, pride, fear, daring, but all she could feel was anger that Bertram had betrayed her.

She could run the estate on her own; she knew how and had the loyalty of her tenants. She did not need a man to help her. The people respected her, she had good workers. The law was unjust; the world skewed to male heirs and she, even though her father had protected her in life, had been left so vulnerable. She stood up and lifted the lid of the small trunk at the end of the bed. Her cousin thought she was about to travel to London and would be expected to take what finery she had. Therefore, she did not have to take two outfits. She would have to take a larger chest to make her departure convincing to Bertram. He must not suspect that she was returning. She did not want to weigh the coach down if speed was of the essence. Parthena decided that she would half pack it and leave her other belongings stacked in the smaller trunk and left in her cupboard. He was not likely to check.

She stared out at the land and her heart felt lighter than it had for a long time. She would not be facing a lonely life as a governess at some family's beck and call. Instead, she was going to marry a man whose purse she had stolen — albeit he reclaimed it, but in its place she was really beginning to believe she had unwittingly stolen his heart instead. The thought filled her with more hope of happiness than she had had for the last year. At her loneliest and most desperate moment, he had appeared to her in the midst of the night as she had crossed a lonely street to find shelter behind an inn, hoping there was a stable she could hide in.

Fate he had called it; destiny was a better word, she thought. However, her heart he had yet to win, for Parthena had learned that men were capable of great darkness when they were presented with new wealth, land and opportunity. He was giving up his freedom and yet he would benefit from it. She did not intend to be one of the benefits, not unless his heart was truly pure, and that she would only discover when she became Mrs Jerome Fender.

Chapter 14

Parthena entered the dining room and saw that Bertram was already talking to Jerome, who was hovering by the fireplace, looking up at a painting of the estate.

Jerome turned to face her as she entered and she could see he was impressed by what he saw. In order to act the part of a female who had had her head filled with talk of finery and London society, she had chosen her best evening dress. A finely embroidered petticoat flowed over white silk, giving an ethereal quality to her movements. With a bodice adorned with gold flowers and ornamented with a deep magenta thread, and her hair arranged high with hanging ringlets she knew she struck quite an image of refinement.

"Oh good, now we can eat," Bertram announced, pulling out his chair and sitting down. "Come, Jerome, no time like the present. We're starting with a simple poached fish — trout, I believe, fresh from the river. Sit, Parthena, I have had Hubbart split yours, dear, as we must look to keeping you as youthful in appearance as we can — gluttony sits badly on a young maid's hips."

"I do not think that Miss Munro has any such concerns," Jerome stated, and shook his head slightly to Parthena to advise her not to rise to Bertram's ill-conceived words.

"Odd setting, three, but my apologies, Jerome, there was no time to invite more. Charles has left town already and society women are few and far between around here." Bertram reached for his glass of wine and waited for the first course to be served.

"You look divine, Miss Munro," Jerome said, and pulled out a chair for her.

Bertram looked up and smiled when Jerome winked at him. "Yes, glad you made an effort, cousin. Almost made the wait worth it," he added, his eyes focusing on the fish as it was carried in. Betsy, a maid, was serving it, as he had dismissed all the male staff when he arrived, except for the stable hand and the footman.

"Who is Charles?" Parthena asked innocently.

"No one who would interest you, my dear. He is a business associate of mine. Now, tell me about your sister, Jerome?" Bertram blustered. "What was it you were saying about her?"

"She is beautiful, like a butterfly, and as delicate," Jerome replied, but his eyes were watching Parthena.

"How so?" she asked.

"She has always been so and is sensitive by nature. She is not as hardy as some, but do not misunderstand me for she is no weakling."

He spun a tale of a lovely lady, and Parthena found herself almost believing his words and feeling empathy for this poor, fragile Eleanor who was about to be exposed to the bartering of the marriage market. The parallels to her own situation were not lost on her, even if Bertram was ignorant of them.

She glanced over the silver phoenix centrepiece of their dinner set, amazed that Bertram had not yet started selling off the family silver. This particular piece had been one of her father's favourites. The bird rose from the ashes and offered up light from the candle's flames.

She watched Bertram whilst her plate was taken away and the main courses were arranged. Bertram had not pulled back from trying to impress Jerome. A roast beef replaced the centrepiece, then a game pie and apple tarts were placed around it with a simple dish of buttered turnip and one of pickled vegetables. There was enough food on the table to feed at least six. Bertram's eyes were locked in on the pies. "Help yourself, Jerome, a man should, as he knows his own limits." He then picked up Parthena's plate and placed a sliver of beef, a small cut of pie, a spoonful of turnip and a limited selection of pickled vegetables on it and then placed it in front of her.

"Thank you, Bertram," she said, fighting to keep the edge of sarcasm from her words. He then piled a wedge of pie on his own, with beef at the side. These he accompanied with a small spoonful of buttered turnip. "Men need meat!" he offered as his final words of wisdom. He gulped down a glass of her father's best wine and had it refilled. She was poured a half glass and a full glass of lemon cordial. Ladies were not used to alcohol, or should not be, he announced, before having his own refilled again.

Jerome ate a sensible amount of the entire fayre. She ate slowly, listening to Jerome and watching his manner, as Bertram nodded and refilled his mouth at regular intervals, speaking whilst still chewing.

When, at last, Bertram was done eating, she expected the sweet course to be placed on the cleared table. But Bertram's extravagance had apparently come to an end. A selection of simple candied fruit was placed in the centre.

Parthena knew that she had to accept Jerome's offer. He was attractive and she owed him, but did not relish being 'owned' by him or any man. He had behaved as a gentleman before he knew about the inheritance, yet, as she had listened to his words, he seemed to revel in this new persona he carried off so well. She could not help but feel slightly disturbed by how easily the lies slipped off his tongue. How eloquently he took Bertram in, and therefore a niggling doubt gnawed at her:

what, she wondered, was the truth of it? Could it be that Jerome was somewhere between the man she had met in Gorebeck and the one that he portrayed to her greedy cousin? It would make him more real, less of a hero. Would not that be better than having someone else she placed above others in her affections like she had with her father? After all, even he had thought he had her future safely covered, not trusting her to make judgements herself and look where that had left her? She was not angry at him — she never could be, but she now realised that he had shortcomings and faults too. Her father, like the rest of mankind, had not been infallible.

"I wonder…" Jerome looked up suddenly at Parthena and then at Bertram. He paused.

"You wonder what, man? Just say it," Bertram said, impatiently, and then forced a guffaw out. "State your mind, Jerome. Any friend of Charles is a trusted friend of mine."

Parthena glared at Jerome out of Bertram's distracted vision; she did not want him to overdo his part. He obviously enjoyed toying with her cousin, but she knew Bertram had a wicked temper and could throw a tantrum when he did not get his way. Patience was far from his nature.

"May I make a very bold suggestion, Bertram?" Jerome asked.

"Please do!" Bertram replied, rather too quickly.

"If Miss Munro is agreeable, would she be allowed to come to London and share the Season with Eleanor? With your blessing of course." It had taken two courses of good but fairly simple food to reach this point. The dinner had been most frustrating for Parthena and obviously excruciating for Bertram. She had wanted to ask Jerome so much about his actual life, his world, his family, and instead had had to endure an evening that felt more like a game of charades.

She had thought of many questions to ask about this proposition to her, but found herself listening as a bystander as Bertram asked many instead about her care, the arrangements. "Of course this will be a considerable cost to the estate. I mean the gowns etc.," Bertram said, as if he too were believing the lie.

"No, you misunderstand me; the cost will all be mine. I shall have my wife and Eleanor take her to the best lady outfitters and she will lack for nothing. It is the least I can do. After all, you are saving me precious time trying to find a suitable companion for my sister. My wife does her best, but she has other relatives and social commitments to attend to, and Eleanor demands a great deal of her time."

"Well, Parthena, it turns out you are a very lucky girl!" Bertram said, quaffing his last glass of dessert wine before making ready with his port and cigar. He had not even asked her if she would go.

"Forgive me, Mr Fender, but…" she began, as it did not seem appropriate that she would accept so keenly, without question. Bertram may think on it later and realise it was all too convenient and equitable. Somehow she had to make it his decision that was once again forced upon her.

"But nothing… I think that it would be an excellent opportunity for you, Parthena. After all, you will only waste away in this backwater. Time is not a good friend to women and you are no longer in the first flush of youth," Bertram said. He looked at Jerome and nodded as if he should agree.

Had he ever looked in a mirror! The balding, podgy, infuriating little… Parthena's cheeks began to burn, her temper near to breaking point, but then Jerome's voice cut across her thoughts.

"I assure you that I will take excellent care of you, Miss Munro. As a man of the law you can take my word as binding," he said and smiled, but his eyes conveyed concern.

She smiled in return and raised her glass. "Very well, I would like to propose a toast to the lovely, Eleanor. I hope we spend some very happy hours together." She finished her wine in one gulp and then stood up rather too quickly, but managed to maintain her composure. "If you will excuse me, gentlemen, I have much to prepare. When shall we be leaving, sir?" She deliberately looked at Bertram. "Are you sure you can manage here without my help?"

He glared at her. "I have no doubt. You will leave in two days' time!" he stated.

"I have to get back to my offices," Jerome explained and shrugged apologetically.

"Goodness!" Parthena exclaimed, as she dropped her serviette on her empty plate and swept out of the room. "I must be swift in my arrangements."

After Parthena had left the room, Jerome retired with Bertram for another drink, fists clenched and jaw firm. He had seen mightier men than this buffoon, Bertram, fall. If he could knowingly cast Parthena into such a trade and still eat, the man was below contempt! Jerome would bring the might of justice down on him with a heavy dose of revenge. Bertram had signed his own sentence, Jerome would willingly treat him as harshly as the man had planned to treat his ward.

Jerome continued his guise and talked to Bertram of the beauty of Vauxhall Gardens, of Boodles and Almack's Assembly Rooms. The smokescreen that he had created for Bertram had worked convincingly. He continued to question Jerome about his intentions. How soon would Parthena be 'away'? Would he entertain her in London for a time himself? There was to be no mistake, she must not return. Jerome said that he would seduce her en route, so that she would willingly obeyed his will. Bertram believed all of his lies and it was amusing for Jerome to behold such a simple mind as his.

Parthena watched from the window of her bedchamber as Jerome left. He walked with great speed down the short drive to the gates that opened into the village square. Who was he really? A saviour? A gentleman? Or a clever cad? Whoever he really was, he was her future and Bertram's end. Bertram would have to crawl his way back to his Mama, defeated by a woman and her friend. If ever an injustice was done in this world it was that men had gained an upper hand in the balance of nature, and the resulting effect on the lives of countless women had been dire. How many in her situation ended up as governesses, companions, or worse, made to feel as a burden in the household of their brother's family with no future of their own — dependent on marriage. She could not change the ways of the world, but she would change her own future and if, when this was done, Mr Jerome Fender turned out to be a disappointment, then she would think long and hard about what to do next. For she would not settle quietly anymore and wait to be told what to do.

Chapter 15

The next morning Parthena heard Bertram shouting for Elsie Hubbart to fetch his coat and hat.

"Going to the village, Bertram?" Parthena asked, as she came down the stairs.

"Never you mind. You should be in bed, resting, for you'll need to make sure that you're at your best when you travel to London," he said, and could not stifle a guffaw.

Parthena looked at him and smiled innocently as if she did not know his dark secret.

"You are very thoughtful, cousin. But I am so looking forward to seeing Mr Fender's sister that I could not possibly languish in bed. I have so much to prepare for."

"Carry on then," he said, and marched quickly towards the coach.

Not long afterwards, Mr Stanton arrived as planned. Parthena was waiting near the door for him, so that he did not need to alert the servants of his presence. He looked as though he had walked at speed, his wavy hair was quite unruly, but he was not short of breath. He carried with him a leather document case. Looking at it, Parthena wondered if it held the secret that would unlock her future and save her and the estate.

"Welcome," she said, opening the door before he had the chance to raise the knocker. Parthena had sent Elsie out to collect eggs from one of the tenants and the maid to fetch fresh herbs from the walled garden.

"Miss Munro," he said. "I am so relieved to see you here and looking well."

"Why ever would I not be?" she asked and stepped aside so that he could enter. "Mr Stanton, I am so glad that you have taken the time to see me," she said and smiled. She took an instant liking to him. His face looked fresh, his eyes kind and his manner humble rather than arrogant.

Parthena gestured that he follow her. These were strange times, so propriety was no longer something she worried about. Parthena was more concerned that the next two days passed by without incident. If all went well then beyond the wedding they would claim the inheritance; if all did not, then she would be married and totally dependent on Jerome, a stranger, and the estate would fall with her. Once in the day room she closed the door firmly but as quietly as she could. "So, Mr Stanton, I understand you have a gift for me from my father." She saw the look of relief on his face. He, too, wanted to get straight to the point.

"Yes, I have." He promptly produced an envelope from his leather bag. "This was for you for your twenty-first birthday, Miss Munro."

"I thank you for keeping this safe for me and for my eyes only." She took it, and then apologetically replied, "I have not offered you any refreshments…"

"There is no need, Miss Munro. I do not wish to be found here by your cousin, either." He smiled. "Is there anything you would like me to assist you with before I leave?"

"Yes, there is," she replied, as she read the short note. It simply said: *Take care of your time, my dear Parthena, and use it wisely!*

"Ask away." He stood watching her.

"Tell me, Mr Stanton, is Mr Jerome Fender a genuine and honest man?" She stared at him as she anxiously waited for his reply. "Is he a man of his word, and has he my best interest at heart, or only yours and his?" Even to her ears her question seemed naive at best and pointless at worst, but she was a keen watcher of people and she looked to see his reaction more than listened to his words.

Stanton nodded without hesitation. "He is, Miss Munro. I would stake my own reputation on it. I knew him some years ago, before the wars, but he was an honourable man who I looked upon as a friend, with great admiration. He saved me from many a thrashing at the hands of lesser people who were supposed to be learned. I do not think you would find a better man, and I believe he has your best interest at heart. War changes people, but I believe that a truly honourable man remains so."

"Thank you for your candid answer. I am in a very difficult situation, you understand."

Stanton nodded. "I am afraid that I do," he said.

Parthena was relieved and judged the man to be honest, as he had kept her personal gift away from Cousin Bertram for so long.

"Then please bear witness to my using this key, as it opens a door inside the clock's case."

"Of course," Stanton said and stepped aside. They went out into the hall where the grandfather clock stood.

"It's a Dumville longcase clock," she explained. "Father's pride and joy," she added, as she used the key to open the panel in its base. "My father had this compartment especially made. He would keep what he called his emergency fund in there." She crouched down and pulled out a velvet pouch and a leather wallet. "Oh, look!" she exclaimed as she found an emerald ring, necklace and matching earrings all delicately set in fine gold work. "They are exquisite!" With them was a short letter which simply wished her well and to be as proud of the person that she had become as he was of her. Parthena swallowed. He was a man of few words but those words were always precious and wise.

The wallet held notes to the value of two hundred pounds and the final document was the deed to the school house in the village. A further message was left with it stating: *You will always have a home in Leaham, should you need it.*

"He left me the school house. The first floor of it has living quarters and the attic is a study room that overlooks the salmon course and the river. He wanted me to have some independence if I was not married, or welcome at the Hall anymore. If he had only realised the type of man he had left the Hall to he would have made better provision for everyone, of that I am sure. But for all his generosity it is nowhere near enough to save the land from my cousin's plans. Please, come with me, and I will show you the drawings in Bertram's study." Parthena locked up the clock case again, carrying her precious belongings with her.

"It is a great help to you, but it is by no means a vast sum, Miss Munro." Stanton's words drifted in the air as she walked on, and in her heart she knew them to be true, but she had never seen so much money in front of her — money of her own, before. She had always bought things on her father's account in the village and he settled them for her. What need had she had previously for money?

Parthena walked over to the desk and nodded to the file. Mr Stanton opened it and began perusing the detail of the plans and she saw a look of horror appear on his face.

"If this goes ahead, the estate, the village, my home, will all be ruined." He stared at her. "This cannot be allowed to happen. It has to be stopped, or the biggest travesty ever to befall this lovely place will unravel!" His colour had heightened with the passion in his words. "Forgive me," he added, "I know the cost of this is heavy on your shoulders, should you choose to act to save us all."

"Unless I marry before the end of the month, to a man who I hope that I can trust, and who will help me to foil Bertram's plan, then yes, all is lost," she said.

"Yes, that is so," Stanton confirmed. "It is a lot to ask of you and I have no right to intervene, but if you would do this, I will be your friend and advisor for free for as long as you need my services. I would do everything in my power to see you were not … that all was well with you and the estate…" His words drifted off and they stared at each other. "On that I give you my absolute oath."

"Thank you, I could certainly do with a friend at the moment and the promise of a life-long one should never be cast aside lightly," Parthena replied. "Then I will bid you good day, and when next we meet I shall be a married lady. I will be Mrs Fender." She held her head proud as she replied, but inside she was shaking at the thought.

"I wish you well, Miss Munro, and I thank you from the bottom of my heart. This is a sacrifice that must be difficult, but the alternative of being under Mr Munro's charity would be far, far worse. You see, Bertram Munro owns the land that the school house is built upon and therefore could still charge you land rent and squeeze you out to demolish it to build some of the mill houses." Stanton closed the file and they left the room as they had found it. "You would be at his total mercy and I believe that he does not know the meaning of the word."

"I know, but I have been given a solution and now you had better leave before Bertram returns and his suspicions are raised, or one of my servants begins to ask questions and gossip amongst themselves. We must be seen to abide by Mr

Fender's outrageous scheme. Your friendship is valued already, sir."

"Good day and I wish you every happiness." Stanton replaced his tall hat and stepped down, but then turned to her before she had the chance to close the door. "Miss Munro, be reassured, for Jerome is an honourable man. I would trust him with my life, and I am sure that he will cherish yours."

Parthena watched him go, clutching at her things and, once he was out of sight, summoned Elsie.

"Yes, miss?" Elsie said, as she appeared from the servants' corridor.

"I need your help. I am to pack for a journey to London," Parthena explained, as she began to climb the stairs to her room.

"Another journey so soon?" Elsie repeated. "My, you are certainly full of surprises, miss!"

"Yes, Elsie, I am. It seems that destiny is putting all manner of surprises across my path." She glanced back at her life-long servant and saw worry and concern on that familiar face.

"But what of the Hall — of our future here? You've just returned and…" There was a note of panic in Elsie's voice and Parthena stared at her. It was Elsie's life too, she had a right to know, but it would be a folly for Parthena to share her plans at this point. She wanted to tell Elsie that all would be well, but she dared not.

"Elsie!" Parthena said sharply and the woman smacked her lips together tightly.

"Sorry, miss," she said and began climbing the stairs after Parthena.

Parthena stopped without looking at her and said, "Have faith, Elsie, things are rarely as grim as they seem."

Bertram blustered into the inn where he had arranged to meet with Jerome. It was a quiet village with a small tap room, although it had a built-on lounge area to accommodate the coach travellers who stopped for a change of horses here.

"Good to see you again, Bertram," Jerome said, as the man took his seat.

"Are you all ready to depart tomorrow?" Bertram asked before he had time to even place his hat on the settle next to him.

"Ready and waiting. I do like a bit of sport," Jerome added and took a swig of ale.

"Good, good," Bertram said and looked at him. "So, what was it you wished to see me about this morning?"

Jerome had been mulling over the same question. He had to have a reason or the man may rush off back to the Hall.

"You say you have property in Kent?" Jerome decided this was as good a starting point as any.

"Yes, I have an estate on the outskirts of Tunbridge Wells; Mother is in the habit of taking the waters there. She swears by them and stays at the mansion when she can — at least once every spring and autumn." Bertram smiled.

"So you will sell up that property too?" Jerome asked.

"Yes, once this sale has gone through. Why? Are you interested in expanding your properties in Kent?"

Jerome could almost hear him adding up the possible profits to be made.

"I am always looking for opportunities," Jerome said, and sat forward. "Tell me about your property."

"Mother's grandfather was a man of the cloth. He had a good living from his parish in London, but the air there was no good, dirty place, you know that," Bertram chuckled. "As a bishop he could give her father a decent parish and living in the country. Of course, he lived with us for a time. His parish continued to do well under a curacy, a man he paid well enough. Then unfortunately he died. Such a fine man. Bishop Dilworth was given a very grand send off, but alas it was not long after this that my father-in-law died too. I was still at boarding school, but my dear mother was strong enough to survive the dreaded ague that had taken her loved ones."

"Pleurisy?" Jerome asked as his mind whirled around. 'Dilworth', that was no coincidence; the local reverend must be a cousin or some close relative. No wonder they were in this scheme together. "Tragic, indeed your mother must have a strong constitution." Jerome realised she was about to need one. He would bring Bertram to justice, but he would not see a broken-hearted old lady left in diminished circumstance even if she had raised a poor excuse of a man. "Where are you going to get your workforce for here, once the mill is built?"

"Well, the Irish are good builders, I understand, but Charles will see to organising that as his part of the development. He has a man who will oversee it and once the machines are in then he will fetch young women from the cities: London, Liverpool and Manchester. The Irish he will send back." Bertram sniffed.

"So you will bring these young women in and their families?" Jerome continued.

Bertram was becoming restless. "Of course not. If they have families to tend to then how will they have time to work in the mill?" He leaned forward. "Charles sends out his men to recruit them. Young and cheap you see. Saves them from a life on the streets or in a workhouse. Orphans are usually good stock apparently. Used to discipline and, once scrubbed, he has a doctor check over them and then sets up his mills. He has them fed two meals a day and arranges for some basic education and then they are seen as benevolent institutions. They are sent to work elsewhere once they reach a certain age as we do not want any families." Bertram took a swig of his porter. "I really have nothing to do with this. My aim is to secure a sale, see to the transition and, once the mill has been established, I merely collect a modest share of the income as an ongoing fee for my part in the sale of the land. By then my attention will be back in Kent." He smiled but his face froze as he realised how much he had told Jerome. "So, would you like to visit Maldon House? It boasts a very good aspect overlooking the downs."

"Does it have good stabling?" Jerome asked to hold Bertram's attention.

"Yes, and is on the main route to Hastings, so excellent for a man wanting to go to London or the coast."

"Yes, I would very much like to see Maldon House, when our business here is done," Jerome said and saw a very happy Bertram order another drink so that they could toast their good fortune.

"So, if you found a new supply of young girls from London, would that help you in any way?" Jerome watched as Bertram's eyes almost twinkled at the thought of yet more coinage heading his way.

"It might, but I must return to Mother and Kent. My part here really is transitional."

"Yes, yes, I understand that, but once I have aided you with Parthena, perhaps you could come to London with me for a visit. You see, I am a benefactor of a foundling home, and we are always overcrowded. They are not all illegitimate. In fact, it is quite common for families to give children over because they cannot afford to feed them as their families grow."

"Ignorance of the common man!" Bertram snapped. "They rut like rats! I tell you there is a natural order in this universe and it is up to gentlemen like you and me to see that it is kept." He swigged his drink.

Jerome's grasp on his tankard tightened. He had served alongside such 'rats' and found them to be of the very best of men in a crisis. Even Wellington had allegedly called them the 'scum of the earth', yet wars were won or lost by these men. Personally he had found them more useful and reliable than some of his fellow officers, who had little idea of what to do when faced with live combat.

"Would you be interested?" Jerome asked. He desperately wanted to spin out the time so that Parthena and Stanton were not discovered.

"How much a head?" Bertram asked. "If Charles is to be impressed we would have to come up with a good price and then of course allow for our expenses. Are they sickly?" he added as an afterthought.

"No, the nuns look after them strictly, but well."

"I shall tell Charles about it and if he is interested then..."

"I thought that we could perhaps share a drink in Boodles?" Jerome said, trying to add honey to his lies again. "Wait till you have visited and seen them for yourself. Then you can give the man hard facts."

At the mention of Boodles Jerome saw that he had Bertram in his palm.

"Of course, why not. I am due a respite from my responsibilities here. Perhaps we could arrange a date for my diary."

"Let me see to Parthena first, and then I will send a coach for you and you can come and join me." Jerome smiled.

Bertram could hardly believe his ears. "A coach?"

"Yes, we have one in my Mayfair house. It is a small luxury, I know, but my wife enjoys its use when we are in town and it serves to help impress some of my peers." Jerome sat back, glancing out of the small window. He saw Stanton was returning to his offices opposite and instantly felt lighter in spirits for he had had quite enough of Bertram's company. Now he had set his trap for the man he could go back to rescuing Parthena.

"And why not? A lady of refinement like my dear mother knows these things are of great import. We could take a turn around Hyde Park or the Mall, could we not? I do not ride much these days — my gout you understand."

Jerome nodded. "You must excuse me as I have to make arrangements for my journey tomorrow. Make sure that your cousin does not have a turn of heart. I do not want to waste my time."

"Absolutely. You have promised me that she will never return, and I am willing to take your word as good and honourable." Bertram stood and shook Jerome's hand.

"She will not, so there need be no connection between you from the moment she leaves in that coach."

Bertram excused himself, making straight for the Hall.

Jerome waited a few moments, watching his figure as it shrank in the distance. He needed to gather his thoughts and once he had suppressed his anger he left and walked over to Stanton's office.

"Did all go well?" he asked, as he entered.

Stanton quickly shut the door behind him and nodded. Briefly he explained what Parthena's father had left her.

"What troubles you so, Geoffrey?" Jerome asked, as he sat down.

"Her future, our future, relies wholly on her marrying you before Bertram can find out and attempt to stop it."

Jerome nodded. "So?"

Stanton shook his head. "Jerome, I believe she holds doubts."

"About me?" Jerome asked.

Stanton nodded again. "Bertram has proven to be a wretch of a man and of course that has shaken her. Even her father's lack of vision, which left her in this predicament, has, I believe, rocked her trust in men. Now she is faced with marrying a man who is almost a stranger to her. It is a lot for a young woman to take on and with no time to think any of it through."

"That is understandable, but I will have to change her mind and calm those doubts. She will do this for her land and tenants. I know her enough to guarantee that," Jerome replied, but his heart was also troubled. He did not want her to harbour any doubts as to his character or motives.

"You too will be married, Jerome. This you must think on with equal measure because it is not so easy to cast off a young wife for no reason. I worry I am wandering to the wrong side of the law in helping you in your intrigue."

"Then don't agree with my plans. See your world crumble around you. Explain to your wife that you could have helped prevent it and then turn Parthena over to a man's guardianship who would have her sold into oblivion!" Jerome's voice was deliberately terse.

"Forgive me. I cannot do any one of those things, as you know." Stanton smiled.

"Good man, but now we have some work to do that does not concern Parthena at all." Jerome stood up. "I want information on Bertram Munro and Maldon Hall, Tunbridge Wells, also Bishop Dilworth and his son-in-law, a Munro, another priest, both deceased, and their connection to your present reverend. Bertram is the latter's son, as his mother was a Dilworth. I am going to bring him down to London in a few weeks and I will need answers by then. Can I use your office for an hour to send off some letters of enquiry about his affairs? Tripp, I cannot touch, as he is no more than an immoral opportunist who hides behind the face of progress, unless, in time, I can find proof that he is finding and abusing his young workforce in any way." Jerome suddenly had a thought that made him look pained for a moment.

"What is wrong?" Stanton asked.

"I have to write one more letter, to my mother," Jerome said and swallowed.

"Port?" Stanton offered.

Jerome walked into the town square, and suddenly had the uneasy feeling of being watched. He saw a dark figure slip smoothly inside the small church on the edge of Leaham. He was dressed as a priest, but he had been lurking on the street opposite and then slipped away in a hurry. Jerome also saw the Munros' servant woman, Elsie Hubbart, leave the grocers' and make her way back to the Hall. Interesting, he thought. It seemed that eyes were everywhere today.

He decided it was time to go to the church and become acquainted with Reverend Dilworth.

The church was quite small. Its windows were not highly decorative and the pews were old and plain. The stone floor gave testament to the centuries of feet that had walked over it.

"Mr Fender, isn't it?" A man appeared like an apparition from behind a stone column.

"You have the advantage, sir." Jerome faced him and noted his sharp nose, like an eagle's beak, he thought.

The man held a Bible in one hand. He stretched out his other and shook Jerome's hand with surprising firmness. His eyes kept Jerome's in his sight without flinching. Jerome guessed they were of an age, which surprised him because he thought Dilworth to be an older man.

"Forgive me for being so presumptuous, but this is a small town and there is little that happens within it that I am not made aware of." The man's lips were smiling, but his eyes were not.

"Really?" Jerome said and glanced around, looking to the vestry door which was open. Had this man been watching him, or had he met with Elsie Hubbart in the town? The sooner that he and Parthena could leave this place the better. It may get back to Bertram that Jerome had been in Stanton's offices. However, as they were both men of the law perhaps he could still bluff the man should he challenge him over it. Small towns had too many watchful eyes; anyone new or acting outside their normal habits raised interest.

"Yes, it is a heavy load, sir," the man remarked.

"Why would that be?" Jerome asked.

"Well, the death of Mr Munro, which will inevitably bring in changes, the reappearance of Miss Munro, and now we are blessed with your presence," he broadened his smile, "like a guardian angel, rescuing her and taking her back as a companion to your dear sister. How I wish I could travel with you and see Miss Munro safely to her destination."

"You certainly do seem to have an ear to the ground. But tell me, you refer to Miss Munro's disappearance. I understood that she had just returned from a visit to her old Abbey School, to see the nuns." Jerome watched the man place the Bible down on the back of a pew and fold his arms.

"Do you?" he remarked.

"Yes, but it is of no consequence." Jerome tilted his head slightly. "It is a shame you did not travel with her, then you would have seen her safely to her destination yourself. They may have welcomed you warmly," he added.

To this comment the man raised his eyebrow. "Indeed!" He stood straight, his arms dropped by his side. "I wish I could have, but I was not here at the time."

"Sorry?" Jerome was confused. It was not often that he was so thrown off-guard. Did the man lie — in church?

"Reverend Dilworth was covering the parish, whilst I was in York on ecclesiastical business."

"You are not Dilworth?" Jerome echoed.

"No, Mr Fender, I am not." Those startling eyes had registered Jerome's surprise.

"Who are you then?" Jerome asked. "And where is this Reverend Dilworth now?"

"My name is Reverend Trevor Mountfield. Reverend Dilworth has retired back to Kent to be near his cousin. His health suddenly declined."

"So what interest do you have in Leaham?"

"I was expecting to be sent on an overseas mission, but instead was … persuaded to return here. For the time being, my new mission is 'pending'," Mountfield replied. "So I am trying to save souls in this small town of Leaham instead of in the heat of the Tropics amongst native people who have not yet heard of our Lord. It would appear there is a greater need here."

Was that sarcasm or bitterness that tinged his words? "This is not a permanent living then?" Jerome asked.

"Temporary. But, tell me, sir, why are you here?" Mountfield asked back.

"In the church, or in Leaham?" Jerome fired his question as quickly as Mountfield had his.

"Both." Mountfield leaned against the back of a pew, facing Jerome.

"You have a very abrasive manner, sir, for a priest, if you do not mind my saying so?" Jerome deliberately sounded haughty as he realised that, depending upon who was the source of the reverend's information, Jerome was either a known associate of Tripp, a confidante of Munro, or seen purely as a rescuer of Parthena. So should Jerome portray himself as a cad, a barrister, or that of a caring friend?

"Perhaps, but I am hearing some very worrying rumours about the village, the property, the people and you … Mr Fender." Mountfield had a very calm manner that Jerome found a little disturbing.

"Well, unless you like talking in riddles, man, I would suggest you stop listening to gossip and state what is on your mind. This is a house of God, is it not? Lies and tittle-tattle don't sit well with Him, so I understand." Jerome saw the colour flush in Mountfield's cheek, though his expression did not change. Jerome had definitely hit a nerve.

"Very well." Mountfield raised both hands palm upwards. "I shall seek forgiveness later. Never doubt that our God sees whatever we do." He relaxed his hands. "Tell me what a London barrister is doing in the small village of Leaham?"

"Visiting a friend. Why are you disturbed by what you have heard?" Jerome countered.

"I spent time in France. I watched a war take many lives and destroy others. There is a smell to a place when all is not as it should be, as there is to some people. I pray that you are an honourable man and would ask you again, why are you here? Are you really an associate of Charles Tripp?"

Jerome shook his head. "I am here as you are, on your own business. I hope that my smell does not come between you and your duty." Jerome was not about to risk revealing his true intentions to this man. If Mountfield knew about Charles Tripp he could be dangerous to Parthena. If he realised Jerome had lied about his association with the man, they may have a bigger problem to solve. Neither was he going to spin any further lies. He had his plan and he would stick to it. The priest would have to just sit and wait, or report back to Tripp if he was in fact in the man's pay.

"I will leave you to your devotions and suggest that you spend your time wisely, praying for your congregation and their future. Good day, sir." Jerome walked away, but could feel the man's eyes boring into his back, so it was with a great sense of relief that he felt the fresh air on his face again.

Jerome realised that he would have to lay low until the coach was ready to depart the following day. The less this man could see of him and his activities the better. Mountfield had not mentioned Stanton, so perhaps he had not seen him in his friend's offices. Time would tell and time was running out.

Chapter 16

The next morning, Bertram's high spirits were almost too much for Parthena to bear. She was frantically trying to look as though she was excited about going on her journey. One she had, supposedly, no intention to return from.

Looking out of the window she saw Bertram talking to Reverend Mountfield outside the Hall. Reverend Dilworth had left before her return and she had not had the chance to form an acquaintance with his replacement. She had just been thankful that she had not had to face the man and lie to him too. Bertram's stance was not easy, and indeed the reverend appeared to be being turned away. Strange, she thought. Whatever were they up to now? The man glanced at the Hall over his shoulder, but walked straight back down the drive at some speed.

"Miss!" Elsie's voice almost made her jump.

Parthena turned around sharpish to see Elsie and the maid Betsy both standing in the doorway.

"What is it?" she asked.

"Mr Munro has sent us to pack up all of your things for you." They looked at her half-filled trunk, and also the garments that she had piled to be stored in the cupboard.

"Well, as you can see I have already started."

"Yes, miss. You are to take the smaller trunk with your immediate things, like you did before, and we are to pack and store your other things for them to be sent on. He insists you rest up and we sort it for you," Elsie added.

"I shall rest here," Parthena sat on the window seat, "and supervise, or how will you know what I want to take?" Aware that they were looking at her curiously, she smiled. "Men have no idea! Here, take that pelisse and store it for me in the large trunk…"

"That seems right, miss," Elsie agreed, and began laying out her clothes on the bed.

Betsy looked ill at ease. Parthena watched her as she placed jewellery in a box and then wrapped the emerald set in a cloth and placed it to the side. The jewellery box was placed in the small trunk but the roll was discretely picked up with two folded shifts and was going to be placed in the large trunk, destined to stay at the Hall.

"Stop!" Parthena snapped her words out.

Betsy nearly dropped the jewels. "Miss?" A look of guilt froze on her face.

"Give me those!"

The girl did so, anxiously.

"Why were you separating them from my other jewellery?" Parthena demanded to know and saw Betsy's eyes well up with tears.

Elsie intervened. "Mr Munro said any fancy jewels should stay here for safe keeping. He saw the ruby necklace when you wore it at dinner with Mr Fender and…"

"I shall take them with me in the carriage in my portmanteau; they shall stay near my person. What else has he had his eyes on?" Parthena asked.

The women shrugged.

"Very well. You will not mention this to him unless you are specifically asked, and not until I have already left." Parthena stood up, having taken her jewels off Betsy. She would not let her father's gift out of her sight until she had safely departed.

Parthena ate in her room and did not come down until the coach was pulling up outside of the Hall the following morning. Her luggage was loaded but she kept her emeralds in her portmanteau which she held on tightly to. Seeing Jerome as he was greeted by Bertram filled her with relief and some level of anxiety, but a bubble of joy welled up in her as he took her hand and led her to the carriage.

Bertram said his goodbyes to Jerome, merely nodding at her before he went back inside the Hall.

The carriage moved and without word the two of them stared at each other as if both wondering who should break the silence first, when the vehicle lurched and stopped as they reached the drive's gates.

The figure of Reverend Mountfield appeared by the coach door. Jerome lowered the window.

"Off to London so soon?" Mountfield asked.

"Yes, was there something you needed?" Jerome replied.

"Give my respects to Jules, Mr Fender."

Parthena looked from one to the other.

Jerome tried not to show how taken aback he was at the mention of his brother's name.

"Jules?" he repeated.

"Your brother, Reverend Jules Fender. We were at the same college and were ordained at the same time. I thought your face was familiar. Although your hair is much darker than his, which threw me off for a while."

Jerome could have hit this eagle-eyed man. What had he been doing digging into his past? Jerome knew only too well that whatever Jules had told this man would be as bitter and twisted as Jules was himself. "I am glad that you are no longer tormented. Is that all? We have a long journey to make." Jerome made to lift the window.

"No, not quite. Miss Munro, should you wish company in London please accept this." Mountfield passed her a letter. "It is in introduction to my aunt. She is a very caring soul. Take care, miss." He stepped back without looking at Jerome.

"Thank you, Reverend Mountfield. I shall send word of my safe arrival."

Jerome slammed the window shut and tapped the ceiling of the carriage with his cane top.

The coach lurched forward and Parthena had to put her hand out and steady herself by grasping Jerome's knee. She soon sat back again and braced herself until the even momentum of the coach returned. Then under Jerome's watchful gaze she opened her letter.

Miss Munro

The man you travel with has lied to you. He is a man of law, but does not have a sister or a wife that I am aware of. Take care and on arrival in York, go to the address below. My aunt will keep you safe until I can come to help you.

Reverend Mountfield

"Well?" Jerome asked curiously.

"Do we travel by York?" she asked.

"No, we would if we were to head to London, but we are going to Whitby."

"Why?" she answered.

"Because to get to Scotland by road would take us days. It would be exhausting and we need to return quickly. Instead, we go by sea up to Berwick and from there a short journey into Scotland. We will be back in less than half the time."

She nodded. "Very well."

"The letter?" He raised a brow as she thought for a moment. "You still doubt me?"

She handed it to him.

"He may mean well, or he may know Tripp. He has no loyalty to the village, Thena, he seeks a life of a missionary. Either way, it is of no import. We go to Whitby," Jerome said confidently, but in his heart he was troubled. The man intended to go to York to collect her. He would find out that she had not been there, not taken up the offer to see his aunt, and that they had not travelled that way. He stared out of the window. The damned man may even follow their trail if he rides! Blast him, whoever Mountfield was, and where his allegiance lay, it would not be with Jerome, of that he was certain.

Parthena placed her letter safely back in the portmanteau and stared out of the window. "I am going to Whitby, then on a journey by sea." She swallowed.

"Would you rather stay in the care of Cousin Bertram?" Jerome asked.

"No, that cannot be." Jerome watched Parthena swallow again. "We go by sea."

Chapter 17

It was after a very rushed journey, at speed, that the coach finally arrived outside an inn in the ancient port town of Whitby. Parthena was shaken by the rutted journey but the majestic view of the ancient abbey ruins on a distant headland had lifted her spirits, along with the sight of the ocean. She had always lived on a country estate and travelled as far as Harrogate and York, but had never seen this beautiful coastline: a totally different sort of wild to the moorland they had just crossed.

Parthena and Jerome had remained silent, each lost to their own thoughts and a little unsure of what to talk about. Three hours had passed by and they descended the steep bank into the town to the noise of the seagulls' kwarking and the sounds of shouts from men working both in the busy boatyards and on the ships, merchants vying to sell their wares and local people milling around the town and harbour.

Parthena realised that she lived a life of luxury by comparison to these people — a troubled one, yet very different to these people who merely tried to survive. It made her resolve even stronger to help her own tenants and the villagers.

Jerome stepped down into the street and spoke with the driver. He paid the man, she presumed for the stabling of the carriage whilst they were on the next part of their journey, and then he opened the door for her and lowered the carriage step himself before offering her a hand to guide her down.

The air was bracing. Parthena discreetly stretched her aching back.

"We have time for a quick repast and freshen up inside this inn and then we must embark upon our next part of the journey." Jerome looked at the driver who was busy talking to another local man, a fisherman Parthena presumed from his attire.

Parthena nodded and held on tightly to her portmanteau as he did his. He led her inside the inn. She glanced up at the angel sign that was its namesake and thought how much she needed one looking over her now, for she had never been in a boat before and the thought terrified her.

"Parthena, there is a rest room there where you can refresh." Jerome pointed to a door at the corner of the small room.

She nodded.

"Wait for me here when you come out and I shall see that our belongings are stored safely."

She gripped her bag. "We are not taking them with us?" she asked.

"That bag and this one, yes." He held up his own portmanteau briefly. "The trunk stays here awaiting our return, like the coach."

Parthena nodded, realising she had not thought this out thoroughly enough, but Jerome apparently had. She was to travel light. Her fear that her possessions were to be stolen was dismissed. She could not show Jerome that she was having second thoughts on the wisdom of this venture.

"Thena, if you wish to change your mind, I will not hold it against you, but you must realise, there is no going back for you. You have committed yourself to this plan — as have I," he said and raised a brow at her beneath his tall hat.

He was handsome, she thought, with strong dark features that were in such stark contrast to her own. She smiled. What a time to have such notions!

"I am not going back to the Hall as Miss Munro, but as Mrs Fender, as we agreed. Now, excuse me, I desperately want to refresh myself." Parthena quickly walked to the door he had shown her as she needed to relieve herself. Knowing that a lengthy boat ride was to come she could only pray that her stomach would hold on to the food they were about to have, because in truth the jolting of the carriage had done nothing for her constitution.

When she returned, he had a plate of mutton stew, a wedge of fresh bread and a glass of wine waiting for her on the table.

She had combed her hair, and washed her face and felt fresh in both body and soul. Smelling the food she realised that part of her problem was that she was very hungry. In her anxious state she had not eaten much before leaving the Hall, which in hindsight had been folly.

They ate their food in silence; it was only when she had finished and sat back in her chair that Jerome spoke.

"What thoughts are running through your pretty head, Thena?" he asked as she sipped her wine.

"Are you sure it is me who is having doubts? This plan of yours hardly compares with the kind of wedding your family would expect of you, does it?" Parthena saw his expression change. Shock, she thought, and her heart ached for she was sure he doubted his gallant, but rash decision.

"Thena, I honestly do not care what they expect. I do not want a marriage that is shallow. I want someone who feels passion for the land they represent, for the life they have and, hopefully, in time for me. I do not wish to live in London, Thena. If you are willing, I would live at the Hall and learn how to make the estate stronger, so that it would never be threatened again. We may holiday in Kent and I can show you where I grew up and also you can meet my mother, brother and other relatives. I will not hide you away, or hide with you. If you are willing… Thena, I want this to be a real marriage."

Her attention was taken by a figure who she had seen ride past the inn's window. "Jerome…"

"Yes," he said, and looked at her intently. She had not heard his words because the man was all too familiar.

"Jerome…"

"Think on it, you do not have to answer me this minute." His hand touched hers and she looked back at him.

"Jerome, we are followed. That man, Reverend Mountfield, the priest, he has just ridden past. I am sure it is he." Parthena watched Jerome's expression change to one of anger.

"God damn it!" The irony of his words was lost on him as he made it clear that they needed to act fast. "We cannot be caught mid elopement by a nosey bloody priest. Of course, Tripp could have sent him, or he could have become inquisitive himself. The man has served in the army. He may well know how to track and how to capture an enemy, or a couple eloping. We have to leave quickly."

He left coin on the table and grabbed his bag. She did likewise.

"Come, Thena, there is not time to waste. We go through the back of the inn and cut across the yards to the harbour. Our boat will be there. Whilst he scours the inns we shall slip away. But we must move fast."

Parthena was led by the hand out of the back door of the inn, across a cobbled yard and past crab and lobster creels, coils of ropes and stacked nets by the harbour. Jerome had looked from behind the inn's walls before they had made the break and seen their pursuer go along the west bank of the Esk, whilst they crossed to the east side. Jerome smiled. "We have made it. If he was to see us at all it will be from horseback as we leave the harbour."

A sailing vessel was further along the quayside and she pulled to run to it.

"No, not that one," Jerome said, and Parthena looked at him puzzled. He pointed to some steps that were bracketed to the harbour wall. She peered down, and saw a fishing boat bobbing about on the water — with fishermen in it staring back at her.

"You have to be brave, Thena. This is our boat and these men have agreed to take us now, but we must away with the tide before the weather turns." He took her portmanteau from her and dropped it down to the men below along with his own and then said, "I will start to go down, you have to climb down them backwards and I will steady you. Once at the bottom step you can jump into the boat and I will catch you — you will not fall."

Parthena nodded and watched as he turned around and began to disappear. Once his head and shoulders were the only parts above the height of the quayside, he gestured she turn around and follow him. "Trust me," he said.

Parthena did and found that a new feeling overwhelmed her beyond that of fear and anxiety. This was becoming the most exhilarating sensation she had ever experienced. She stood in the boat with Jerome's arms encircling her waist, steadying her. The wind on her face was moist, coming in from over the sea; fresh and salty.

"Sit yourself down, lassie, and we'll soon have you away," a seasoned sailor said to her with a bone pipe hanging from his lips as if it was permanently attached to them. Jerome put their bags together and they sat with blankets around them; they smelt funny as Parthena sniffed the wool.

"That smell is because they have a coating from sheep's' wool that will help keep the moisture off you."

They huddled together and she watched as they set sail. The boat was small in comparison to the high-masted ones she saw, stacked with sacks of grain and other goods; they were soon underway. It bobbed along on the water's swell as the men manoeuvred the vessel towards the harbour entrance to the open sea. They saw Mountfield on his horse near the harbour side, but whether he saw them or not was too difficult to tell. Once beyond the safety of the harbour's shelter they left the comparative calm of the river Esk, and the movement become more as if rolling from one watery hillock and onto and over another. There was a steady flow that Parthena found almost mesmeric. It was strangely calming rather than frightening. Certainly after the jolting of the carriage journey as it sped along this was far gentler.

Glancing back, she saw the church on the headland and the ancient abbey ruins behind. They must have been a welcome sight to many a man returning from their trips to see their loved ones again. The sea was busy with vessels travelling along the horizon. She nestled in next to Jerome, enjoying the temporary feeling of peace, until the swell became more apparent. Parthena became aware of the moving mass of water beneath the boat. The men laughed and joked as they rowed, their dialect was in a rough accent she did not understand but they seemed good natured enough. That, she thought, may well have had something to do with the money that Jerome was paying them.

"Do not be frightened, Thena, but sleep, for it will be morning before we arrive. If the sailing is good." He pulled her even closer to him with his arm wrapped around her shoulders.

She let him, for the warmth and the motion was making her realise just how tired she was.

"I am not scared," she said, without trace of a lie. She loved the feeling of being away from the confines of the Hall and Bertram and in this vast watery wilderness, until the swell became waves and the waves began to build.

Parthena eventually slept but awoke in pitch dark as if she had been engulfed somehow by the sea and yet she was not floating, but the ground she was resting on was wooden and wet. She tried to sit up but there was something over her. She panicked and tried to push it away.

"Thena, it is alright. The storm was not too bad." Jerome rolled the sail cloth back and the bright sunshine that flooded her senses made her eyes squint. They were turning from the open sea towards another harbour and the seawater was becoming choppy again.

"Thena, are you well?" Jerome asked her and she smiled.

"I must look a sight and my skirts are wet, but I am fine. Is that Berwick?"

"Yes it is." He sniffed, and she realised that he had wrapped his greatcoat over her and he was chilled. She gave it to him and he slipped it back on. "The hour is early. We will find somewhere to refresh and eat and I will arrange for the rent of two horses. We must cross the border as soon as possible. These men will be back for us in two days' time. Then we will retrace our steps."

Parthena nodded. It seemed to take an age, but she was so grateful to be back on solid ground. Her hair was a mess, her skirts and coat hem were soaked, but her portmanteau was safely with her. Jerome looked as though he had not slept well, but he was fully focused on finding them horses.

He managed to find an inn where they could grab a hot drink and some food.

"Thena, I have brought something for you to wear for your comfort on the ride." He opened his bag and pulled out a roll of what looked like fine cloth. "These are trousers. I got them in a smaller size, but they should do you fine. Go slip them on under your skirt in the restroom. Be quick. The stirrup at the end of the leg slips under your foot before you put your boots back on. They will keep you warm and also protect your modesty as you ride."

"Thank you, Jerome, most thoughtful," she said. They were quite fine and slipped on under her skirt. They felt odd. She almost felt tempted to remove her skirt and just wear the breeches and her coat, and thought she perhaps would on the journey if needed. Right now they had to appear decent as they left this busy port.

When she walked back over to him, she felt as though she stood taller somehow. Was this how men felt, like they could move freely?

"No one would know. Now, we must go," he said and stood up, throwing some coin onto the table to more than cover their bill.

They walked toward the town. "Thena." He suddenly stopped and looked at her as he was about to enter a stables.

"Yes, Jerome?" she asked.

"You can ride, can't you?" he asked.

Parthena saw the look of concern on his face. "Yes, Jerome," she said.

He nodded; the look of relief was plain to see and she smiled sweetly at him. After all, how difficult could it be? she wondered.

She waited whilst he arranged for the horses and brought them out. "I'm sorry they did not have a side-saddle, you will have to be bold yet again and sit astride yours. I asked for a fairly timid one."

Parthena smiled, mightily relieved, as she had no idea how to sit on a side-saddle anyway, so riding like a man should be a lot easier.

"Good, it will be better that way," she said.

With a bag fastened carefully to each animal, Jerome helped her mount her horse and then he did likewise.

When hers began to step backwards and then sidewards instead of forwards like his, Jerome stared at her. She was sitting upright with a rein in each hand and was trying to nudge it forward with her knees. "Go on, go on," she said to its twitching head, willing it to do what she wanted but feeling sadly inadequate to the task of making it do so.

"Thena," Jerome said, as he took the reins from her.

"Yes, Jerome?" she replied, looking very guilty.

"Don't ever lie to me again. Hold onto the saddle, I will lead your horse."

She clung on as he walked the horse through the busy streets until they could take the road away from Berwick and head north to Scotland. Parthena was smiling all the way. She had not had so much fun for years, if ever, when he increased the speed and the horse went from an amble to a bumpy trot, to a canter. He alternated the pace but kept going with only occasional clipped comments on their surroundings from her. Eventually, after hours of constant riding, the fun was wearing off, or her buttocks were.

"We will be in Scotland by late afternoon, Thena," Jerome said.

"I think I can steer the horse myself now," she offered.

"You lied!" he snapped.

"I knew you were in a hurry and did not want to hold us up."

He glowered at her.

"I'm sorry. It was stupid and childish. I always wanted to ride, but father said it was dangerous. He wouldn't let me."

"I am not your father!" he said.

"I know that!" she barked her reply back at him. "If you were I wouldn't be in this mess, because he would still be alive and Bertram would still be with his 'mama' in Kent!" She was almost shouting at him.

He stared at her. "*This mess* being that you are about to marry me!" he said. He held both horses' reins but his eyes were fixed on hers.

"I am sorry. I will not lie to you again. I thought I knew better than I did." Her words were calm and honest.

His gentle manner had gone and he still seemed vexed. She thought he had taken her ruse a little too much to heart, but she had apologised and that was as far as she was prepared to go. He could sulk if he wished to.

He led her horse on. "Apology accepted." He did not look at her but kept his sights on the road ahead. "We ride, we refresh and we marry."

Chapter 18

Reverend Mountfield had no success finding them in Whitby as he rode around the harbour, but he had decided to stay the night at the inn. Asking the stable hand had been the most useful decision he had ever made. The lad would obviously sell his aunt for the price of a shilling.

Having ascertained that Fender and Miss Munro had bought passage on a boat headed north and that they were expected to return from Scotland in a few days time, Mountfield's worst thoughts had been confirmed. Jerome Fender was living up to his brother, Jules', expectations of him. Fender had obviously hoodwinked the pretty Miss Munro and they had eloped to Scotland. The gullibility of females where men and desire were concerned baffled him. His mood was as dark as the weather was turning. Captain Jerome Fender, as was, was a cad and his family would finally have the proof of it.

"I need pen, ink and paper," he said to the innkeeper. "Have them sent to my room." He paid for them and for his dinner, which would be sent up also. "Once written I would like the letters to find their way onto the mail coach as soon as is possible."

The man nodded. "Good as done today, sir, so long as you can have your letter ready in the next two hours."

Mountfield felt somewhat relieved at his decision. Fender's mother was a lady that Mountfield's own mother had spoken highly of. She, at least, would be forewarned. Meanwhile, he would try to find the words to explain to Mr Munro what fate had most likely befallen his ward.

He wrote his letter to Reverend Jules Fender, for it would be best if his suspicions were revealed to the man's mother by the son than from the impersonal words of an acquaintance. Satisfied that he had acted wisely, he passed the letter on to be despatched by mail coach that same evening and went to his bed content. He wanted to rise early in the morning to be away to Leaham.

Mountfield closed his eyes and whispered words of comfort to his own ears, "But blessed are your eyes, for they see: and your ears, for they hear. Amen."

Parthena was both cold and numb by the time they crossed the border into Scotland. If she hadn't been, she might have admired the beauty of the countryside, but it seemed hostile, like Jerome's continued bullish attitude toward her since she had told the slight lie about her ability to ride. They stopped at the first village that they came to. Grateful to find a small inn, they entered only to be stared at like invaders by the local faces.

Parthena looked down at her portmanteau, which she hugged closely to her. She was not afraid of these people, but very tired, sore and hungry. The last thing she wanted was a confrontation.

Jerome talked to the innkeeper and he seemed slightly aloof at first, then he smiled and a sparkle of joy crossed his bristled face. He waved Parthena through to a room at the back of the inn behind the tap room. This strange, dark building smelt of cheap oil, musk, ale and pipe smoke. After all the fresh air that Parthena had breathed in on the journey since they had left Whitby it seemed almost overbearing, but she was warm and felt relatively safe. The fear of highwaymen had crossed her mind ever since they left Yorkshire. Yet here she was in an inn in Scotland with Jerome, being shown a cosy nook of a room, hidden away, with a fire and a small dining table that had two stools tucked under it. She smiled; they were to eat at last and in relative privacy and comfort, away from prying eyes.

"Ye'll be right snug in 'ere." The man winked at Jerome and nodded to Parthena as he opened what looked like a cupboard door to reveal a built-in bed behind it. Well, thought Parthena, she could find it comfy, but Jerome would have to find his own cupboard to curl up in, for his was hardly roomy enough for two, even if she considered allowing him in with her.

"Very well, this will do nicely," Jerome said and shook the man's hand.

"Aye, ye'll sleep like babes," the man said, "even though I've never tried it masel', many who taken the vows an' slept in't an' we've had nae complaints so far." The man chuckled then beamed a smile at them both. "I'll have the missus stoke up a fire and bring ye some warm food to fill yer bellies. And I'll fetch the Father for ye, nae worries. Ye'll make a fine looking couple that's for sure. The wee yins will be guid looking tae, ye'll see." He nodded at Jerome. "We're better than any blacksmith's anvil here and we give good food too!"

Jerome did not say anything until the owner had left them alone.

"This place is quite a find, is it not?" Parthena asked, and saw both of Jerome's eyebrows rise.

"You think we merely stumbled upon it?" Jerome shook his head.

She bit her lip to stop words of anger from flooding out. Of course Jerome knew where they were going and what they were doing. Yet, she had never done anything so daring before and it was all scarily new to her. "My apologies again," she said, but stared at him so that he knew that her heart was far from behind the words she uttered.

"We are tired. We have travelled far and it has taken slightly longer than I anticipated due to the slow progress of our ride..." Jerome began.

"Oh, for goodness sake!" she snapped her words, uncontrolled and heartfelt. He was trying the patience of the saint that she never claimed to be. She folded her arms and stood in front of him. "Do not be so churlish as to sulk like a wronged child. I lied to you only to try and speed the journey up, as obviously a gig would not be safe on these roads. How was I to know that riding was, well, more difficult than it looks?" She was taken aback when he laughed in her face, yet was grateful that it broke the detached atmosphere that had formed between them since they had arrived in Berwick. Then, as suddenly as his outburst of mirth had begun, it ended.

"I will not tolerate lies, Parthena! Not from you. You are to be my wife. You have to be honest with me if we are to work together through this."

"I explained why I did it and I apologised to you for it! What else do you want of me? Or are you still angry that I stole from you?" Her hands were now on her hips and she was staring him down, or trying to.

"My, my, Miss Munro, you have quite a temper, do you not? I shall have to watch myself, or I shall be a hen-pecked husband." He placed his hat on the table and ran a tired hand through his hair before pulling out one of the stools and sitting tiredly down upon it. "Did you apologise? Oh yes, you did, for stealing my money and that has been accepted, but you must see that I cannot and will not abide untruths. We must have transparency between us or we will fail in this venture, and in life."

"This venture?" she repeated, still trying to contain her anger with this infuriating man. His words were filling her head with confusion. She trusted him, she had to, but if he were to doubt her over such a silly boast on her part then what were they to do?

"You know what I mean, do not toy with me. This arrangement, our marriage of convenience — call it what you will, you need my help, Miss Munro, and I offered it freely, so do not reward my trust with lies, even if you consider them to be small innocent ones — they are still beneath you and could have caused us serious delays."

"I am sorry," she said. "I did not realise the impact my words would make."

"And I too need to apologise to you. I have sulked badly, and it is not becoming, is it?" Jerome shrugged and almost smiled. "I have seen much and take the world very seriously. The things your cousin would be a party to, in order to make it easier for him to claim that land is criminal. I aim to stop him, but I have killed and crushed better men fighting face to face in battle. I do not expect you to understand that and I shall make allowances for you. We nearly lost the time we needed to marry here, and I do not wish to stay two nights, or we shall miss the boat back to Whitby. We are at the mercy of the elements as well. This year has seen torrential rain. Even at Waterloo we were nearly washed away before the battle began. But once we have the licence, Reverend Mountfield can do nothing to stop our plans going ahead. Neither, more importantly, can Mr Bertram Munro sell your land to Tripp — it will be mine legally, if not yours, morally."

"When are we going to ask the priest to wed us then, Jerome?" she asked.

"He has been sent and paid for. The 'service' will be no more than a short exchange of vows with the innkeeper and his wife as witnesses. It will take place here, shortly, and then the papers will be signed and legally binding."

Parthena's panic erupted into anger. "I am to marry here! In a small bedchamber, right now, without washing or changing, without time to recover from the journey?" Suddenly it all seemed so real, startlingly so. "We have not even talked about it — you are happy for it to be done, like that?" Parthena felt pushed beyond reason.

"Yes, just like that. And, no, not here. I understand that there is a small chapel — a converted store room, at the back of the building. The priest marries couples there, like they do in Gretna Green. You are fortunate because we have had to come up the east coast and not the west, or you would be married to me in a smithy with an anvil for an altar. Yes, you and I will both be dirty, just as we are, humble before each other and God. It is as we agreed. It is a marriage of convenience. We lost time to 'freshen up' as we could not ride freely and at speed, so brush your hair now, or do what you need to, but we will be called in minutes." He stood up and took a step over to her. Placing a hand on each of her shoulders he looked solemnly into her eyes. "Parthena." His sigh seemed tired but there was a granite rock of determination in his eyes. "You did not answer my question in Whitby before you saw Mountfield pursuing us. This arrangement has to be so; we have discussed that and agreed to it. In time, however, I want you to acknowledge that I hope we will have a full and happy…"

"There ye are, sir, come now. We'll be needin' to hurry!" The innkeeper appeared at the door and was waving his hand frantically for them to follow him.

Parthena was shaken. Jerome eyes flashed anger at the man. He dropped his hands to his sides, looked at her and shrugged his shoulders as if trying to shrug off his mood. "Come, let's get this done."

She swallowed and followed him. 'This' was to change her life. There would be no easy way out of it. He was a passionate man, she could tell that, and if he did not see his way to divorcing her and freeing her, then she would be tied to him for life. This was never to be a romantic wedding, it was rushed and it was for a cause, to save her estate, but she had not envisaged it being in a draughty old store room with a cross placed on an upturned barrel for an altar. Then there was the countenance of her intended. Far from being caring and considerate of her, or romantic, he seemed to be tying himself in a knot with inner turmoil and she did not know why. Unless he was deeply regretting offering himself up. Would he want to have mistresses? Would she care? Could she let him and then claim grounds for a separation? Never in her wildest dreams had she envisaged going to her wedding planning her divorce.

Parthena heard the words spoken around her — to her, by the priest who looked dour but smelt of whisky. His words were either heavily accented or slurred, she could not decide which. Parthena almost pulled away when the priest took her hand but then realised he was giving it to Jerome. She heard Jerome's voice swearing to be her husband and she repeated the words given to her and swore likewise. Jerome took her hand and a gold ring was placed upon her finger. It was only slightly loose.

"Yea are now man and wife! Kiss her," the priest said and did not wait to wish them good fortune, health, happiness or even good day. "Right, I hae signed the licence, there 'tis and if ye want a duplicate I can give ye twae for a fee." He pulled a funny expression with his tongue pushed behind his lips before adding, "Irate relatives can sometimes destroy the first licence they see. Better tae have a second legal document to keep safe; the wedding still holds even if the paper be destroyed."

"Yes, we'll have a copy made. I can see the wisdom of it," Jerome said. He had barely brushed his lips against hers. Money was exchanged again and the innkeeper and the priest handed papers to Jerome and then left.

Parthena tried not to feel as if it was she who was being sold and purchased. Jerome looked at her. "Come, Mrs Fender, we have a long journey again tomorrow so let's be abed!" He took her hand in his, smiled and led her back to their cosy little nook of a room.

"Mrs. Fender, How strange it sounds to my ears." Parthena had thought aloud, as if saying it would help him to understand the speed of events had indeed shaken her.

Food was brought to them and they ate their supper in silence, as they had in the coach journey which had begun their elopement. Parthena found it all a bit daunting — she had eloped!

Sitting on the edge of the bed with the cupboard doors wide open he pulled off his boots. He placed a wallet and a knife and pistol under his pillow.

"If you have anything of value I would put it at the side of you or under the pillow. You will be between me and the wall." He stood up so that she could climb in.

She took her emeralds and purse from the portmanteau, which was placed next to his by their sleeping area.

"Could I sleep on the edge side, please?" she asked, noting that he had not undressed, save for his greatcoat and boots.

"No, you may not." His answer was stark and she felt rebuffed.

She bit her lip. Emotions and tiredness were threatening to overwhelm her. Parthena felt trapped as badly as she ever had, even by Bertram. The feeling of exhilaration and freedom had dispersed on the wind, which seemed to be gathering strength outside the small 'chapel'. This wedding would help her out of her situation with Bertram, but also achieve profit and security for Jerome Fender and his good friend Mr Stanton. One would own a wealthy estate; the other would secure his home.

"If you sleep on the edge of the bed, Thena, and by any unfortunate circumstance we are interrupted by unpleasantness, how would you stop them? You can see that I with knife and pistol to hand that would at least give me the opportunity to afford them a damned good fight whilst you scramble out to a place of safety to obtain further help."

"You think this place is unsafe, Jerome?" Parthena asked and stared at the door that led back into the inn.

"Thena, we were pursued to Whitby. Our business here will stop powerful, bad men from having their way and nip a fortune in the bud. I would rather take precautions, wouldn't you?"

She nodded. "You are not undressing?" she thought and then realised the words had slipped out of her mouth without her brain having the chance to stop them.

"Do you want me to?" he said in quick response, and his face looked more animated than it had done since he touched ground in Berwick.

"No!" she said, rather too quickly. "I was just stating a fact." She pulled off her boots and crawled in the bed. Her skirt was left on the chair but she still wore the breeches. Once she was nestled in, still wearing her blouse and waistcoat fastened up, she breathed in slowly as he pulled the rope that shut the door to their cupboard and they were cosy, in the dark together.

"Try to sleep," he said tiredly.

"Good night, Jerome," she said, hardly daring to move.

"Good night, Mrs Fender," he replied.

Chapter 19

Parthena had lain there for what seemed like hours. She did not know what to expect when the wooden door closed, let alone what to do, so she had done nothing. That included not sleeping. At one point she bit her lip and clung to her rolled-up coat. Never had she felt so confined and yet there was something reassuring about being in a safe closed space. She had used her coat as a comforter; with tears welling up inside she closed her eyelids as tightly as possible. This was the only wedding ceremony she would ever have, this was her first night with her husband, they were man and wife and yet they had not shared a kind word between them, let alone one kiss. Not in friendship or … or like a man should kiss his new wife. They were as two strangers in one cramped bed. It was not what she had envisaged. The tears rolled silently down her cheeks, they were shed out of disappointment, grieving the loss of what she had hoped would be a love of her own, an expression of passion between two souls who would live a life together and truly know each other… Not a marriage of convenience in a hovel with a seemingly regretful and angry man, who clearly wished he had never set eyes upon her, except for the slight sweetener of her father's lands, which were now his. Realising she was in fact very tired she tried to think of happier times. It was hard, as those memories added to her present feelings of isolation and loneliness, but in the trying she must have drifted off to sleep, because the next thing she knew was that her world had been shaken again. The door of their 'bed-cupboard' was flung wide-open and the inn keeper stood before them.

"What is it?" Jerome asked, as he pointed his pistol at the surprised man's face.

"Put that down, sir. 'Tis only me! I cam tae tell ye that your horses are safe and dry, for noo," he chuckled at this, "but ye'd make a swift departure. 'Tis coming in bad and that the weather is travelling doon country."

Jerome stood up at this news. Parthena saw his expression darken. "There's hot oats on the table and coffee for ye. A nip o brandy for the lassie tae, she'll need her strength for your ride." He chuckled again, but Jerome looked down at him and the man sobered instantly from his jocular attitude. "Aye, well, I'll be leaving ye to it."

Jerome put his pistol in his belt and pulled on his boots.

"Was there a storm? I didn't hear anything and I wasn't asleep for long," Parthena asked. She swung her legs down and pulled on her own boots. She could quite get used to wearing breeches.

Jerome rolled up her skirt that had spent the night on the stool and tossed it over to her. "I would put that in your bag. Travel in the breeches and your coat. It will be easier as you are about to get a thorough drenching."

He turned to look at her when she stood in front of him wearing her coat over her blouse, waistcoat, breeches and boots. His eyes seemed to take in her whole form as they looked down before meeting her gaze. "Thena, you are going to have to be brave because the weather has turned. We will ride, as fast as we can, on one horse leading the other. When we get to Berwick, we will hope that the sea has not become too rough for the boat to meet us. This weather is foul and dangerous. You will be wet through for most of the day and you will not be able to dry out properly, possibly until we get to Whitby. Now, eat your porridge and I will see to the horses."

It was only when Parthena went into tap room to find her way out and to rejoin Jerome that she realised just how much of a storm was raging. They had been sheltered by the rest of the building, truly cocooned for the night. The rain looked as if it were coming down in silvery rods. Jerome appeared, rounding the corner of the building with the horses. He was already drenched with water running off his hat and down the back of his greatcoat. He took the bags from her and fastened them to the saddle of the back horse.

"You sit in front of me, Thena, on that one and I will shelter you as much as I can." He was almost shouting at her over the noise of the rain's pounding on the roof above her head.

She nodded.

"Good, come!" Just before she moved, he turned to her quickly and bent down slightly, giving her a lingering kiss full on her mouth. She felt the rain on his skin as he savoured her lips and she his. When he stood straight again she felt the cold after the heat of that all too brief, intimate gesture. He then placed a wide-brimmed hat on her head, and grinned. "If I did not know otherwise I would never suspect you were a woman with that on, let alone my wife. Come on, we must brazen this out to the end!"

She was unsure if he meant the journey or their marriage. There was something about Jerome that she would like to explore further, but there were also so many aspects of him she did not understand. Time would show which of the sides of his personality and promises were real. But she sensed and tasted his passion; he was not as cold and aloof as he behaved most of the time. Perhaps that is what happens to soldiers, she wondered. Do they put on a façade, like a decorative folly to appear more than or less than they actually were? As Parthena stepped out into the rain and felt the strength of his hands around her waist, lifting her onto the horse, she hoped he would reveal more of his true nature to her.

Mountfield arrived in Leaham in the early afternoon. There was a storm threatening and the air was moist and oppressive. He rode to the church first to make sure that all was well there. When nothing seemed to need his urgent attention he gave his horse over to the inn and then made straight for the Hall.

Elsie Hubbart greeted him when she opened the door. He genuinely liked Elsie Hubbart, she had a good heart and fed him well. She was always dropping off a few scones, a cake, some ham to the church, often with a bit of news.

She was walking him into the morning room, when she suddenly changed her mind. "What am I thinking of? You should wait in Mr Munro's study; there's a fire lit in there. It's right cosy, he doesn't like the cold you see. Says it stops him thinking clearly."

"Very well." Mountfield took his cue from her. "You best tell Mr Munro I am here as otherwise I may be in for a soaking on my walk back to town." He smiled at her but her eyes were darting everywhere. This woman was bursting to tell him something, but what?

"Now, we couldn't have that. I'd have Jake fetch you back in the coach if that's the case. I'll tell Mr Munro you are here. Would you like some tea and a slice of my freshly baked cake?" Elsie Hubbart asked. Some of her usual manner had been reformed.

"That would be most kind."

"Well, you stay here, make yourself at home." She glanced at Bertram's desk, which was scattered with papers and plans.

"I'll fetch a tray to you. Mr Munro won't be long. He has just awoken and so he may take a few moments to be down. Perhaps at the very least fifteen before he leaves his room."

"Oh!" Reverend Mountfield was most surprised. "Is he ill abed?"

"No, he likes the port you see. He has more than his fill of it after his dinner and does not rise early unless he has a meeting." Elsie Hubbart seemed on edge again. "You make yourself comfy and I'll see to that tray, and then I'll make sure that Mr Munro is aware you are waiting. I'll be right back." She looked directly at Bertram's desk again before leaving.

Mountfield smiled, subtlety was not her forte, but he was definitely intrigued as to why she wanted him to peek into Mr Munro's affairs. Mountfield sat looking at the plans for Leaham Mill, and the rough sketches for the back to back houses of 'Tripp Town'. He stood up. What on earth was Munro thinking of agreeing to this? The drawings, the letters of intent to sign over the Hall, the tenancies, land, river rights, mining and building rights; in essence everything to Tripp by the end of the month for a princely sum. Mountfield sat down again. "Oh God!" he said, and his expression froze. He was all for progress, but not for the annihilation of a whole village. This place had existed from before the Doomsday book. Had Jerome Fender seen these? For the first time he doubted his own thoughts about the man's motives at taking Miss Munro. Was he another callous prospector hoping to outbid Bertram Munro, or was he actually trying to save the place?

Mountfield sat back in the chair by the fire. Well, the man's mother still had a right to know that he had eloped and taken a wife. Better to hear from Jules than from the scandal it could cause once word was out.

Mountfield received his tea and cake with a polite courtesy. "Mrs Hubbart, perhaps it would be better if I took these into the kitchen and had a few moments with your good self. Once Mr Munro is down I shall enter again."

"Excellent idea, Reverend." Elsie Hubbart picked up the tray again and led the way back to her table by her own little hearth, looking her own confident self again.

He sat down and waited for her to stop fussing about. "In strict confidence, tell me what is actually happening here, Elsie, for I need to know who I can trust."

"Very well, Reverend Mountfield. I'll tell you the little I know, but it is troubling."

Mountfield nodded, sipped his tea and ate his slice of parkin, whilst she began her tale.

"The young miss was sent away. I suspect that something was wrong with the arrangements because no sooner had she left than the trunk that Mr Munro was to be sent on to her was stored in the loft. Then, Miss Parthena arrives back — been looked after by nuns, she says, as the family she was supposed to govern had gone on, or some such. Now that was perplexing enough, but then this man Mr Jerome Fender pops up. He claims as he is an acquaintance of Charles Tripp." She folded her arms, pursed her lips and shook her head.

"How would you know that he isn't?" Mountfield asked, intrigued by the woman's deductions.

"Because he didn't come into Leaham the way he told Mr Munro. My cousin Cecil knows. He works the turnpike and them two, Jerome Fender and Miss Parthena, came back together and split before Leaham."

"Interesting," Mountfield said and finished his tea. "So you do not think his arrival was a coincidence?"

"Nope, besides, we heard Miss Munro and Mr Fender whispering something about saving the village when they took a turn around the garden — right under Mr Munro's watch," she chuckled. "It was only a snippet of chat, but whatever they were planning it was for all of us." She smiled. "Then next they're off, and now you are here wanting to see Mr Munro. So, Reverend, may I fetch him down; have you something to share with him? Forgive my being so bold, but I'd hate for him to worry unnecessarily." Her hands were nervously gripping her apron on her lap.

"No, Elsie, I think we should just let matters be and I am sure that whatever is happening here, we should trust the good Lord to have a hand in it and allow events to unfold. Let Mr Munro take his rest, for he may well need it. Thank you for the cake and your time … and trust."

"If you can't trust a priest, then who can you? Oh, did I mention that it was the Reverend Dilworth who persuaded Parthena to take the post as governess and who put her on the coach — that was just before he left and you arrived."

"No, you didn't, but I am glad that you have, and I assure you that you can trust this priest."

Mountfield left by the back door and walked slowly down the drive, wishing he had spoken to the inquisitive Elsie Hubbart before he had put pen to paper.

Chapter 20

"Oh, Jerome, can we stop?" Parthena shouted. Her horse was beginning to stumble, as the relentless rain was turning the road into a muddy stream.

"There is a small inn just over that rise. It is no more than a shared home, but I doubt that there are many mad enough to travel on a day like this, Thena. We will see if they will put us up." Jerome was shouting his words out as the wind was whipping them away, his mouth so close that she felt his lips touch her ear. They were in a sorry, cold state.

"What in hell's name are ye doing oot in weather like this, and the lassie is fair bedraggled!" the woman who greeted them said incredulously.

She took the two bags that Parthena had been holding and bustled her inside. "You see tae the nags," she ordered Jerome. "My man's aroon the back, he'll set ye right." Jerome did as he was bid. "Come, come." She helped Parthena off with her wide-brimmed hat and coat and looked more than a little surprised at seeing Parthena's legs clad in trousers. "Whativer next? Ye young lassies will be growing beards and smoking pipes soon!" However, she carried on fussing about her and by the time Jerome entered Parthena was wrapped in a blanket and being given a hot toddy as she sat by the fire. Her boots were drying out to the side of the small stone hearth.

"Ye want ye head wringing like that coat, young man!" The woman continued to rebuke Jerome, but as she did, she took his coat and hung it by the door with his hat. His boots were placed next to Parthena's and he too was given a blanket and a drink.

"We offer nothing sae much to heat ye through 'cept good broth. There'll be porridge for ye boith in the morn and ye sleep up there," she said, and pointed to a ladder that had been placed against the wall, which disappeared into an open hatch in the ceiling. The roof space seemed to be the guest room. Parthena was dismayed at the thought, but she was drying out, and with inner warmth wafting through her as she sipped down her drink she was hardly going to refuse such generously offered hospitality.

"Thank you very much Mrs...?" Parthena said and smiled.

"Aye, well I would nae put a cat oot on a night like this, although twas a close call when I realised ye was English." She laughed at Parthena's face as she was unsure if she meant it or not. "Mrs McKenzie, is ma name. Aye, there was a time that ma granny would not have admitted that. Ne'er mind, I'm a Christian and ye are definitely in need a saving."

"Hush, woman, and give your patter a rest." Her husband entered. He too was soaking. "If ye dinnae mind we'll take the payment noo and then leave the twae o' ye. We'll be in the back room should you need anything other than a good rest. Food will be brought in an hour and then at daybreak — that's if daylight breaks!"

Jerome found his coin and his voice. "Thank you, we are very grateful."

The woman nodded and she and the man, happy to have made any money on such a stormy day, retreated to their room.

"It isn't what you planned, is it?" Parthena said.

"Well, if the weather is this bad for us getting back to Berwick then I doubt the boat has made it up the coast either. We'll see what tomorrow brings. We have many days yet to make our way back. But the sooner we can then the more of your home there will be to reclaim."

They stared at the flames of the fire, huddled together on a settle, like two old cronies in blankets, and then they looked at each other and both laughed.

"You have been doing really well, Thena, but we will need to keep going tomorrow."

"I know, or your sacrifice will have been in vain."

She saw him raise a challenging brow.

"Thena, I tried to make it clear to you in Whitby and again back there that this 'sacrifice' is one I am prepared to make… I want you to think about it too… I want…"

"Here ye are. Since when dae I need an hour to prepare some simple wholesome food? It may not be the fine fayre ye be used to, but 'twill keep ye warm!"

"Thank you," Parthena said as Mrs McKenzie placed the tray on the table, nodded at Parthena's appreciation and promptly left them alone again.

Parthena had grabbed hold of Jerome's clenched fist and cradled it in her hands on her lap before the woman could see that he looked fit to explode. She could hardly keep her face straight as the frustration within him was so great. He was struggling to control his temper as every time he tried to speak openly someone interrupted them.

Once Mrs McKenzie left she realised she was still holding his hand, his fist had relaxed and now he was happily holding hers.

"Do you know what it is I am trying to say to you?" he asked.

"No, but if it is that you made a mistake, then…" she swallowed, "I'm sorry for that."

He cupped her face in both of his hands and inched close to her. "That is far from what I am saying. I want you to be my wife, my real wife, that is," he said, finally and simply.

"But I am, am I not?" she said, watching those lips of his seek hers. His touch was gentle to begin with, but then firm as his kiss deepened.

"Now do you understand?" Jerome said, almost in a whisper.

"Yes, I think so. You want me to be intimate with you as if we were truly in love?"

She saw him blink. For a hardened soldier she was surprised to see that he had a vulnerable streak when she was direct with him; sometimes he appeared to be almost hurt.

"That is what you mean, isn't it?" she asked again.

"Thena." He still held one of her hands. "Men and women do not need to be in love to have intimacy. There are many arranged marriages that are like this."

"And you would like this kind of arrangement, between us?" she asked. She wanted more than that. For that pretence would in time, she was sure, be laid bare and hatred would replace the void that lack of love had left.

He let go of her hand and stared at the flames. "There was a time I could honestly answer you, 'Yes', but I have wanted so much more than that ever since I returned from the war. Thena, I may have just taken the legal right to you and all your father owned, but you have so much more that you could share than material wealth."

"How so?" she said.

"Thena, you already have my heart. What else do you want?" His words were filled with emotion.

She leaned into him and kissed him with a passion she had no idea that she possessed. They embraced like true lovers, until he pulled away.

"Mrs Fender, we should seal our marriage properly, I think."
He looked to the ladder to the loft above and was almost
laughing as he spoke, but then a serious note returned to his
voice. "Do you agree?"

"That way no one can call it a false sham, can they?" she
whispered.

Parthena sent him up first with the lamp. It was not as
dismal as she thought. Instead of a grim roof space it was a
room with a low ceiling and wattle walls, and it had a reduced
four poster bed with a board above their heads. The warmth of
the cottage below made the temperature quite pleasant.
Standing facing each other he slowly slipped her waistcoat off,
after quickly discarding his own and the shirt beneath. In the
dim light she could make out a few scars that had healed well
on his firm, tanned torso.

He then sat on the bed and pulled off his own boots, shortly
followed by hers. Next he loosened his breeches. She could
not avert her eyes. He waved a finger at her teasingly and then
undid her blouse. He tossed it onto the one chair that the
room had and then it was his eyes that were transfixed as he
looked to the curve of her breasts that were only supported in
a simple short corset.

"No shift, milady?" he said quietly.

"The skirt was in the way of the breeches so I removed it."

She was almost unaware of his movement as he undid the
lacing, it was only when her corset slipped loosely down her
arms revealing her breasts that she knew what he had so
skilfully done. Parthena held his gaze, she was his wife, for
better or worse and right now it was feeling 'for the better'.

There were no more words. Their breeches both lay on the
floor at the side of the bed. Her senses were alive and every
part of her longed for his caress. Overwhelmed by waves of

strange and all-consuming sensations that she could never have imagined, she let her body control her mind until both lay entwined and exhausted from their sated lust.

By morning, Parthena was Mrs Fender in every sense of the word and she did not regret her elopement for one minute. Her dream may not have been to have a marriage in a tongue she could not understand, in a state that would shame a tramp, and to spend her first day being soaked by rain, and then to be bedded in a hay loft but, as she smiled up at Jerome as he dressed, she was filled with the sense of adventure. Somehow this marriage would be one of equals — at least in their eyes.

She fumbled with the lacings of her corset and pushed all thoughts of his familiarity with the intricacies of a woman's apparel from her mind. He may have lived the life of a bachelor before, but now Jerome Fender was hers and no one else's.

Her moment of reverie was broken when he leaned over and kissed her one more time and placed the rest of her clothes by her side.

"You had better dress quickly, Mrs Fender," he suggested, before he descended down the ladder to see if breakfast had been brought out.

They sat facing each other. "To our long and happy union," he said, and toasted her and she did likewise. "I want to tell you, when we go back to Leaham, we will not only stop Bertram Munro in his tracks, but we will bring the man low. He would have as good as taken your life by taking your freedom. He will pay dearly."

Parthena did not hesitate to reply. "Then let him be brought low. He cared not for how many others' lives he would destroy to pay for his own lifestyle. He needs stopping."

"Very well, shall we, Mrs Fender?"

"Let's," she replied, finishing her last spoonful of oats. She then dug into her portmanteau and handed him a half crown.

"Whatever is this for?"

"I owe you that for I gave that amount to the abbey and it is time I paid my debt in full as I promised."

He smiled ruefully. "Very well," he said pocketing the coin.

They left after bidding the McKenzies good day and facing the storm again, although the worst seemed to have passed by for now.

"No regrets?" he asked one last time before he lifted her onto the horse.

"None, Mr Fender, I promise," she said.

"We ride," he said. Huddled in his arms they did and this time they did not stop until they got to Berwick.

Jerome was right about the boat, it was late arriving, but they managed to meet it and with little time to spare were off on the tide.

When many hours later they rolled into the Angel Inn in Whitby it was all Parthena could do to climb the stairs. She dozed and was only awoken when Jerome said, "Thena, there is a hot bath in the small room next door."

Without further comment she walked straight into that bedchamber, dropped all her clothes and slipped into the lifesaving water. This time, Jerome had no need of mirrors and she no hint of embarrassment.

In the morning, fully refreshed and dressed as a lady again, she would return to Leaham and face Bertram Munro.

Chapter 21

Parthena and Jerome arrived by carriage in Leaham's square by midday. They made straight for Stanton's office to hand over one of the marriage licences.

"I must congratulate you! I really hope that you both will be happy, but at present the important matter is that you are now the owner of Leaham Hall and all that goes with it." Stanton looked to Jerome, and Parthena could not help but resent that. It was theirs, not only his!

"Did you inform the debtors where Bertram Munro is?" Jerome asked anxiously.

Stanton shrugged his shoulders. "It appears that he has used funds from selling off some of the livestock and other readily convertible assets to clear his debts. He may be a buffoon, but he is one who has a knack of surviving the storm, rather like you two." He smiled at them, but Jerome's face, like Parthena's, showed his disappointment.

"Those assets were not his to sell!" Parthena snapped her words out trying not to sound bitter, but she was.

"Well, because he was in charge of the assets as your guardian until we married, he was acting on the right side of the law, as far as he and anyone else was aware. He was not to know you would wed. He may be going back to Kent with his tail between his legs, to a disappointed mother, but he will not be going to debtors' prison! Damn the man!" Jerome admitted, angrily.

The mail coach's horn announced the arrival of the post in Leaham. Reverend Mountfield greeted it as he was anxious to see if there was a letter for him from Jules — there was! Guilt gnawed at him. He had interfered in affairs that he had not fully understood. His thoughts were interrupted when he noticed the bullish figure of Bertram Munro walking as quickly as his portly figure could move to also pick up his post.

"Morning," Mountfield said.

"Letter for you, Mr Munro." A young lad handed it to him from the despatch, but if he was expecting a tip he was soon to be disappointed.

Munro's face was all excitement and animation as he snatched it from the perplexed giver. But his expression froze as he stared at the writing.

"Is something wrong?" Mountfield asked.

"It's in Dilworth's hand, not Mother's as expected," he said and ripped it open in the street. The scream that resounded from the man's mouth made Mountfield and the horses of Jerome's coach start.

Stanton looked down at the street from his office.

"What's happened?" Jerome asked. Jerome and Parthena stared at the strange scene and watched Munro being taken into the inn.

"Has he taken a fall? Did the coach catch him?" Parthena asked.

"I have no idea," said Stanton. "Wait here. I'll see what has occurred."

Patiently they waited for what seemed like an age. Their peace was only disturbed when they realised that Bertram Munro, Mountfield and Stanton were arriving in the adjoining office.

Bertram's almost incomprehensible voice was bemoaning his ill luck. Parthena and Jerome slowly opened the door.

"Mother's dead!" Bertram bawled like a child, waving the crumpled letter in his fist.

Carefully, Reverend Mountfield eased it out of the man's hand.

Stanton was trying to give Bertram a sherry, but Bertram hit his hand, spilling it down Stanton's immaculate trousers. Stanton was far from amused.

"Reverend Dilworth has written to inform Mr Munro that his mother passed away peacefully in her sleep. Funeral arrangements are being made and he is invited to attend. He sends his condolences and informs him also that he is happy that he has inherited Leaham Hall for a home, as he will be returning to reclaim the family estate his sister and Bertram appear to have been managing whilst he was serving the good Lord elsewhere."

Bertram spluttered an obscenity. "I am left to this cess-pit!" He looked at Jerome and Parthena. "What is she doing back here?"

Jerome explained, "This is Mrs Fender, my wife. We now own Leaham Hall, the estate, the tenancies and everything associated with it."

"You bastard!" Bertram yelled. "I trusted you and you lied to me!" He hurled himself toward Jerome, but Stanton put out a foot and he fell headlong on the carpet at their feet.

"You would have seen me ruined!" Parthena said.

"I would have seen you dead!" Bertram spat out his words.

"Restrain him," she said. The men looked at each other. "He needs to be seen by a doctor, he is clearly not fit to be roaming loose."

Understanding her meaning the men nodded at each other.

"Goodbye, Bertram," Parthena said and walked past him to the door. "I will leave you in the capable hands of a priest and two men of law. With a doctor's assessment, I am sure you will receive the care you deserve."

Parthena began walking back to the Hall. The ground was wet under foot but the rain had temporarily abated. Elsie Hubbart came down the drive to meet her. Without words they hugged.

"Are you alright, lass?" Elsie said.

"Yes," Parthena smiled. "I am."

"Is it over, miss?"

"Yes, Elsie, it is. Pack up Mr Munro's things, he will not be needing them. I am Mrs Fender now," she added, liking the sound more and more.

"Are you happy?"

"Yes, I believe I am. However, I am tired and hungry and in need of a wash and change. The coach will arrive later with Mr Fender's things. Elsie, we have been fortunate here, but with the weather, the uncertainty over the menfolk's' livelihoods and all the returning soldiers, this is going to be a trying time for all. We must protect Leaham and make sure our stores are full."

"Aye, and you and your man will. I'll see to all the rest, you go and await your husband." Elsie walked briskly back to the Hall with an energy and bounce in her stride that had been missing for months. Parthena suddenly felt very tired. She paused and looked around her at the land she loved. A few minutes later Jerome placed an arm around her shoulder and pulled her to him. She closed her eyes and hugged him like she would never let go.

"It was the only way he could serve a proper sentence. The man is clearly evil or out of his mind. Women have been placed in asylums for a lot less, so why not him?"

"That is very true and there are asylums that are strict, but not as abhorrent as Bedlam." Mountfield's voice surprised them both.

Jerome was about to berate him, when the eagle-eyed man put his hand up. "I may have wronged you, Mr Jerome Fender, when I interfered with your plans, but I believe I can help you, at least in a way." He looked at them sheepishly. "You see, Jules is about to arrive here." He took a step back as Jerome rounded on him. "Hear me out, and then if you wish to floor me for my insolence, you may. I have asked him to relieve me of my duties, so I can leave to take up my place as a missionary. I may have mentioned your elopement to entice his curiosity."

"You did what?" Jerome shouted.

"Civility please, there is a lady present." Mountfield was smiling, but Jerome was not.

Parthena watched as the man put both hands up in front of his chest as if praying in his defence. "I may have mentioned you had eloped with Miss Munro," he continued, "because I genuinely thought you were doing something ungentlemanly and I apologise for judging you ill. I am coming to you now because I want something from the Hall — your father's office to be precise."

"You mean the deed in the new territories," Parthena said and Mountfield nodded.

"Well, my father paid fifty guineas for it, but he never got to see it. It could be barren wasteland for all I know. That is why it was not mentioned in the will or as a separate part of the estate — it simply may not exist."

"Then let me go and find out. I can report back to you and, if it is worth the working, I could start a mission there and turn a profit for you at the same time."

Parthena considered his words, and then nodded. "Very well," she said.

She then looked at Jerome who was still festering at the news of his brother's imminent arrival.

"You may collect it at dinner tomorrow when I shall meet Jules. Please invite Mr and Mrs Stanton and we shall discuss it further then. Good day, Mr Mountfield," Parthena said.

"Good day, Mrs Fender, Mr Fender."

Jerome glared at him as he walked away.

"So, I will meet your brother," Parthena said sweetly. "Or were you going to keep me as a dark secret — cosseted away on the estate."

"No, I was not." Jerome took hold of her hand. "However, brother Jules will have practically drooled over breaking the news of my apparent roguish behaviour to my mother."

"Well, we shall meet her and place her concerns to rest. It is not as if I am a pauper, is it?" Parthena said and kissed him before pulling him towards the Hall.

Jerome looked at her. "You have no idea, Parthena."

"Oh, I think I do," she said as they entered their home and their future together.

A NOTE TO THE READER

Dear Reader,

Thank you for choosing to read *For Richer, For Poorer.* I hope you enjoyed following Parthena and Jerome on their adventure to seek moral justice.

The Inspiration

Parthena and Jerome cross paths in unusual circumstances. If Parthena had not been sent away to her ruin, or so her cousin thought, they would have made a good society match for each other. However, as a woman whose family home had been left to the next male heir, a greedy and unscrupulous man — her destiny was changed. In desperation she makes a choice to 'borrow' from a stranger in order to survive. From that moment on there is no going back for her.

Jerome is a man returned from a bloody war and has been changed by this stark reality. All that he valued, the superficial, before he left has little meaning to him. He seeks to find a soul mate, a life partner, and to feel the earth solid beneath his feet again. His beloved country is suffering as men return broken and changed to eke out what living they can.

Parthena and Jerome are two strong characters who join forces to stop a selfish and wicked man destroying one small part of the land they love and in the process wipe out the livelihood of a whole community.

That passion grows and transcends their cause, enveloping them as they travel north to Scotland. Not in the more usual manner of a frantic dash by coach to Gretna Green, but by a Yorkshire coble by sea and then by land.

The Early Nineteenth Century

The early nineteenth century was a period of great conflict and change: a time of war, pressgangs, and extreme social, agricultural, religious and political changes. All these impacted on the ordinary people who were left behind, whilst the wars with Napoleon dragged on.

The government taxed its people harshly, whilst still fearing the possibility of a revolution as had happened in France. It was hardly surprising then that smuggling and opportunists abounded, yet in plying the trade they gave coin to an enemy. Some gangs were known for their violence, others were less so and merely supplied a ready market that crossed over social rank and was often funded by a moneyed man.

With the onset of the Industrial Revolution and the growth of new money, lives were changing and the old money was feeling threatened.

The countryside was changing as mills were being built and cottage industries suffered, along with their communities. The population gravitated to these places of work and life in the countryside changed.

In the cities 'society' had strict rules: influence and connections were so important.

In my stories the settings are more remote. These influences mean nothing when a character is dealing with survival, either their own, or someone who they have met. So boundaries are crossed, rules of society are broken or are made irrelevant.

The Region

Most of my titles are set in an area of the country that I love: North Yorkshire, with its beautiful coast and moors.

In *For Richer For Poorer* the old stone trods used by centuries of feet to cross open moorland feature in Parthena's escape.

This would be dangerous and deadly to a person who was not familiar with their path as the boggy moorland that they traversed was treacherous. The cold, the rain and wind bite into the unsuspecting traveller. The beauty on a fine sunny day can be breathtaking, but in late evening and the darkness of night or on a windswept expanse it would make for a harrowing journey.

I used my fictitious market towns of Beckton and Gorebeck in this story. The latter at this point has its own small mill situated just outside the town.

Love is a timeless essential of life. Throughout history, love in all its forms is a constant: be it passionate, caring, needy, manipulative, possessive or one that is strong enough to cross barriers of culture or faith. When two souls meet in a situation which takes them out of their normal social strata or into a shared danger, a relationship forms as the adventure unfolds.

If you enjoyed reading *For Richer, For Poorer* I would really appreciate it if you could take a moment to leave a review either on **Amazon** or **Goodreads**, or wherever you wish.

It is always helpful to read feedback and I am always interested in what my reader's think, or would like to read next.

I can be contacted on:-

Facebook: **ValerieHolmesAuthor**

Twitter: **@ValerieHolmesUK**

Or through my website: **www.ValerieHolmesAuthor.com**

Love the Adventure!

Valerie Holmes

Sapere Books is an exciting new publisher of brilliant fiction and popular history.

To find out more about our latest releases and our monthly bargain books visit our website:
saperebooks.com

Printed in Great Britain
by Amazon